Mail Order Myth

Book 44 in Brides of Beckham

Kirsten Osbourne

Chapter One

Tabitha Murphy set out on her long walk to the post office in Beckham, Massachusetts, wondering if her life would ever be any different. She worked for a family who lived near her in the rural area south of Beckham, doing anything they needed.

Every day she would help Mrs. Matthews round up her eight children, usually taking one or more with her when she was asked to go on any kind of errand. Today, however, the children were with their father, helping him harvest apples, so she was able to sneak away to the post office without four or five children swarming around her.

When she reached the post office, she saw the older sister of one of her closest friends, Elizabeth Tandy, who had once been Elizabeth Miller. "How are you today, Mrs. Tandy?"

Elizabeth smiled. "I'm doing just fine. What are you up to?"

"Picking up the mail for the Matthews. Thankfully Mr. Matthews took all the children to pick apples with him, so I don't have six of them hanging from my skirt." She brushed a tendril of dark hair out of her eyes. Without the children, she tended to walk faster, and then she looked a mess when she arrived at her destination. She'd rather look a mess than have all the children with her. "I also need to go to the general store after I finish here." Tabitha knew she should be thankful to be employed, but working for the Matthews was difficult at times.

"I'm surprised the Matthews children haven't gotten a terrible nickname like my younger siblings did," Elizabeth said, referring to the nickname her own younger siblings had received, the demon horde.

"Me too! From my point of view, and you know I went to school with so many of your siblings, the Matthews children are much worse."

"Sounds like you need a new job."

"If only I could find a man that I wanted to marry. There just aren't any good men left in Beckham."

Elizabeth grinned tilting her head to one side. "I can help with that, you know."

And everyone did know. Elizabeth Tandy was a matchmaker, sending women to marry men in the west as their mail-order brides. Tabitha shook her head. "I refuse to become part of your mail-order myths!"

Elizabeth laughed. "They're not myths! I've had so many successful matches. I'm sure we could find you a man you'd be happy with."

"I'm not sure I'm even up to trying!"

"Come see me after work today. Let me show you a letter. As soon as it was in my hands, I thought of you, and I was planning to send Bernard out to talk to you about it anyway. Your parents don't need you here, do they?"

Tabitha frowned. "No, I don't think they really do need me, but...I never thought about leaving them either."

Elizabeth smiled. "Come for supper, and we'll talk. All right?"

Tabitha really didn't know what to say. She didn't believe a mail-order bride scenario would work for her or anyone else on the planet. But she felt the need to humor the older woman. "All right. I'll let my mother know as I pass by our house on the way back to the Matthews."

"Sounds good. "I'll see you about six?"

"I'll be there."

As Tabitha picked up the mail, shopped, and walked the long way back to the Matthews, she couldn't stop thinking about the idea of being a mail-order bride. Sure, she wanted to marry and not be working for the Matthews and beholden to her parents forever, but the idea of marrying a stranger?

Would he expect to have a wedding night when they'd just met? What kind of arrangement would it be? What if she traveled to wherever he was by train, and he didn't bother to show up at the station? What if he just left her there, with no ticket for a ride home, and nowhere to go?

Oh, the possibilities were terrible, and she knew she would be the one they happened to. Life was simply like that for her. If she expected to have apple pie for supper, her mother would make strawberry pie which broke her out in hives, and she would forget to tell her what she'd made...oh the scenarios were endless. If something was going to go wrong, it always went wrong for her.

She took one step inside the house and called out. "Mother, I won't be home for supper, but I don't have time to chat. I have to return to the Matthews."

"All right dear. I did recently learn there's a man at church who is interested in courting you. Do you know Elmer Jorgensen?"

"The pig farmer who takes all ten kids to church every Sunday, who obviously hasn't bathed in a month?"

"That very same man."

Tabitha looked at her mother with shock. "And you think this would be a good match for me?"

"I don't see you finding another."

Tabitha nodded wearily. "Thanks for your confidence in me, Mother." She shut the door and kept walking toward the Matthews' house. The order from the store had been large enough that the store owner had agreed to deliver it for no charge, which meant Tabitha's hands were free, other than the mail.

As soon as she arrived at the Matthews' home, she put on an apron, and took the mail to Mrs. Matthews, who was sitting in her rocking chair, staring out the window. "Are you all right, Mrs. Matthews?" she asked.

"I just found out I'm expecting again. My baby is six, and I thought I was finished with having little ones. What am I going to do? I'll need to hire another girl, because you're already overworked, and it's not at all good that I make you do so much." Tears were falling down Mrs. Matthews's face, and Tabitha wanted to tell her she'd just work harder, but she couldn't make the words come out of her mouth. She was overworked. No one should do as much as she did for twenty cents per day.

"I'm sorry life is getting overwhelming," Tabitha said.

"I'll live." Mrs. Matthews brushed her tears away and stood up. "I made lunch for Roger and the children. Would you mind carrying it down to the apple orchard." She shook her head. "Just pray that none of them have fallen out of trees this time. I don't need another doctor bill with a little one coming."

Tabitha happily took the food and left the house. She knew Mrs. Matthews well enough to know she was trying to get Tabitha to take a wage cut, or agree to work more during her time there, but she refused. She did feel sorry for Mrs. Matthews, but she was not about to put her own health at risk to help the stingy woman.

Arriving at the apple orchard, she called out that she'd brought lunch, and the children swarmed her. Mrs. Matthews had wrapped all the food she'd sent into a large quilt, which Tabitha spread out and set the food out in a pleasing manner.

Mr. Matthews tended to be much kinder than Mrs. Matthews. "Go back to the house, Tabitha. I'll have one of the children carry what remains back, though we never have any remains after a meal.

Once she was back at the house, Tabitha was given her instructions for the afternoon. Ten loaves of bread, and while the bread rose and baked, it was her job to sweep and scrub the floors. The house wasn't huge, but it was big enough she should have been given all day for the task, not just part of an afternoon. Mrs. Matthews must have been angry she didn't offer to do more, but Tabitha knew she'd done the right thing.

As much as the idea of marrying a stranger appalled her, she was starting to like the idea of going on an adventure. Sure, she knew the man wouldn't show up, and she'd be left standing alone at the train station, but she could at least see some of the country. Maybe she could go to San Francisco. Or Colorado. She'd heard both were beautiful.

As soon as she had finished making the dough and left it to rise, she swept the floors, her mind still on moving west. Where in the west, she didn't know or care at that moment, as long as she was no longer there, taking care of someone else's cleaning and doing the housework meant for someone else. She wasn't paid enough to do all she did.

As soon as the floors were swept, she washed the dust off her hands, and checked the bread. It was rising perfectly, so she punched it down, formed it into loaves, and went back to work. She'd have to do the children's floors, and then she could get the bread in the oven.

Her day was full, and she was thankful when she was finally finished. It was Saturday, so her work week was over, and she could worship on Sunday. Or sleep. Sleeping sounded better than church, because she was certain her mother would insist on her sitting with Elmer and his children, and she had no desire to get within ten feet of the man.

As she walked back into town to eat supper with Elizabeth and Bernard, her mind was on the type of man she would want to marry. After a day on her hands and knees scrubbing floors, the idea of never having to clean a house again was definitely something she liked. Of course, there were no women alive who didn't have to scrub floors.

At the Tandy residence, she ate supper with the couple and their three children ate at the table with them, which surprised Tabitha. She'd heard that most rich people had their children eat at a separate table. It didn't bother her that the children ate with them, but it did strike her as odd.

While they talked, Elizabeth talked about some of her brides and how happy they were now that they were out west.

Tabitha believed that some people would be happy marrying a stranger, but she didn't believe she was one of them.

"I promise, when you see this letter I received yesterday, you're going to want to respond. There's no way you won't want to."

"All right," Tabitha said, the skepticism she felt coming across in her voice.

Bernard laughed. "She's a hard one to convince, isn't she?"

Tabitha had seen Bernard around town, and she knew who he was, but they'd never formally met until that evening. "I've just never had good luck with anything in my life. I'm sure if I agree to do this, I'll be stranded on a train platform in the middle of nowhere, and will have absolutely no money to return, and I'll have to get a job doing just what I'm doing now but with different scenery."

Elizabeth smiled and shook her head. "You would simply send me a telegram, and I would send you a ticket to return home."

"And my telegram would get lost in a pile of telegrams and fed to pigs somewhere."

"Pigs don't eat paper," Bernard said.

"Only my papers."

"We'll make sure everything works out for you," Elizabeth promised.

After supper, Bernard set about putting the children to bed, while Elizabeth and Tabitha went to Elizabeth's office.

Tabitha took the seat Elizabeth gestured to on the sofa, while Elizabeth sat behind a desk that looked both organized and messy at the same time.

Sure enough, Elizabeth knew exactly where what she needed was, and she flipped to a letter, reading it once more before handing it to Tabitha. "I've never seen you with any of the men who have sent me letters before. This man should be yours."

Tabitha glanced down at the letter and read through it slowly.

Dear potential wife,

My name is Jacob Small, and I live in Lisbon, Wyoming, which is a small town along the border of Wyoming and Colorado. I have a small ranch here, that I'm hoping to grow into a much larger operation. I'm interested in marrying a woman who is willing to brave the west with me, helping me to set up a real home where we can raise our children.

My parents died a few years back, and I have no family left, unless I can find a bride who is willing to join me. I live a good distance from the nearest train station, and the last part of the journey would have to be made by stagecoach, but if I find the right woman, I promise to be waiting right next to that stage coach when she arrives.

I'm looking for someone in her twenties, who doesn't mind hard work and is willing to help me grow my spread. She needs to want children, and I would be downright tickled if she could cook.

I await your reply.

Jacob Small

"He does sound like a pleasant man," Tabitha said. "And I like the idea he wants to have children. And he's frank about the fact that I'll need to work once I'm there..."

Elizabeth couldn't help but note that Tabitha was using the pronoun I when talking about the man. She was going to respond to his letter.

"I'll write to him, but we'll see what he says. If he's as kind as his letter makes him sound, then I'm certain he'll be run over by a bull any minute."

"Make it a brief letter, and we'll send a telegram. That way we can get you on the train before the snow gets too heavy for easy winter travel."

It was already mid-September, and though it was still summer, Tabitha knew the other woman was right. She picked up the pencil and paper offered to her, and quickly wrote a response. "When will I know something?" She wanted away from both the Matthews and her mother who wanted her to marry a pig farmer.

Though she had nothing against pig farmers in general, Elmer and his family were filthy people. She did have something against marrying a man who didn't bathe and who didn't make his children bathe.

"It should only take a few days to get a response. I'll send Bernard out when we know something." Elizabeth smiled. "I like the idea of you going somewhere you can be happy."

"Is it so obvious I'm unhappy?" Tabitha had never thought about whether she looked unhappy to others. Knowing life was hard and not showing it took real effort.

"Not to everyone, but I can see it. Let's change all that, shall we?"

"I'm not so sure a rancher from Wyoming is going to be able to make me into a happy person so easily."

"What good is life if you're not willing to try?" Elizabeth asked. "I'll have Bernard take you home."

"Thank you." Thinking about everything Elizabeth had said, Tabitha decided to make a real effort not to let her misery show to others. Perhaps if she acted happy, she could become happy. Though that was the hardest thing to do.

Chapter Two

J ust three weeks later, Tabitha found herself standing on the board sidewalk on the side of what could be called a street if one stretched their imagination far enough, in the tiny town of Lisbon, Wyoming.

She waited for almost an hour before she stopped the next person walking past, a man in dirty clothes, a crumpled cowboy hat, and boots covered with what she hoped was mud and not something entirely less appealing. And what was less appealing than mud?

"Excuse me, sir, but do you know Jacob Small?" she asked.

The man took off his hat and slapped it against his leg for some reason Tabitha simply could not fathom. "Jacob Small? What do you want with that idiot?"

"Idiot? I'll have you know I'm here to be Jacob's wife!" Tabitha felt the need to defend the man who was about to be her husband, whether she'd met him yet or not.

"You kidding me?" the man asked, looking at her as if she'd lost her mind. "How'd he convince you to marry him? You one of those mail-order brides who comes from the east to marry someone you never met? It's the only way he'd ever get a wife."

"Well, yes, but...he was supposed to be here to meet me."

The man stood staring at her for a moment, and then he simply started laughing. "Jacob Small is a squatter. He lives down by the river, and he has no home. Just lives out in the open. He herds pigs around like they're sheep, but he calls them cattle. I've never seen a man who was more deranged than Jacob." He laughed a little more. "Now, if you want, I can take you to meet him."

"No, thank you." Tabitha raised her chin and met his gaze head on. "Why would you laugh so much at another person's misfortune, Mr...?"

"Blander. Bert Blander." He still looked as if he was ready to start laughing again, so Tabitha did something terribly out of character for her, but necessary for her feelings at that moment. She kicked him. Hard.

"You got my cowboy boot, girl. You didn't hurt me."

Tabitha was so angry with him, both for laughing at her and for being the bearer of news that her future husband wasn't sane, that she wanted to cry. She raised her foot to kick him again, and this time aimed higher, smiling when he shouted in pain when she hit his knee. "Now what am I supposed to do?"

Bert stared at the girl for a moment, wanting to help her despite the fact that she'd kicked him...twice. He watched as she sat down on a bench looking despondent. Instead of going on about his business, which is the thing he knew he should do, he took the seat beside her. There was a trunk in front of her and a carpet bag in her hand.

"Look, lady..."

"I'm Tabitha Murphy." She was mortified to see a tear fall onto her hand, and she kept her face down so he wouldn't see her cry.

"Nice to meet you, Miss Murphy. Now I'm not sure if there's another man in town looking for a bride, but I suppose you could stay with me tonight, and I'll introduce you around at church tomorrow."

"I couldn't spend the night with you! What kind of woman do you think I am?"

"I have no idea at all what kind of woman you are. I do have a live-in housekeeper who is married to my ranch foreman, and they will act as chaperones, if that's what you want."

"They will?" Tabitha peeked up at him, and he saw the tears shining in her beautiful blue eyes, and more tears clinging to her eyelashes.

"They sure will. Do you want to come home with me, and we'll make sure you don't marry an idiot or a man who isn't quite right with the world?"

She smiled at how he categorized Jacob Small. It was better than calling the man an idiot. "You don't mind?"

"I don't mind. Just don't kick me again."

"Then don't deserve it again!"

He sighed. "I'll have to come back in for your trunk. I rode my horse into town."

She frowned. "I suppose I'll have to stay with it then."

"I'm going to the store. I'll be back in a few minutes."

While he was gone, Tabitha could do nothing but fret about her future. She wondered who had sent the telegrams to her because the person hadn't sounded insane, but he must be.

She was thankful Mr. Blander was taking her home with him, and she wouldn't have to sleep in someone's barn or something, but still. She couldn't count on a stranger to keep her forever...or for even longer than one day.

She worried she would end up having to go home with her tail between her legs and beg for her job with the Matthews back, even though she had no desire to work for them again. She didn't even want to live with her mother again. Perhaps there was a seamstress in town who needed another pair of hands. Or maybe she could work at the store. That could work. But then where would she live?

Oh, why had she gone against her instincts and gone to marry a stranger? It made no sense when she knew she was the unluckiest person alive.

When Mr. Blander came back to her, he said, "The store is going to deliver your trunk along with my purchases. Let's go."

She stood up and walked with him, carrying her carpet bag. He stopped in front of a horse and asked if she needed help up. "Where will you ride?" she asked.

"Look, lady, I didn't bring my wagon or buggy into town. If you're waiting for a special ride, talk to the merchant. I think he would let you ride out with his son."

Tabitha wrestled with her decision for a moment, but decided she'd rather ride with the devil she knew instead of the one she didn't. "Yes, I need help up." She'd been on a horse before, of course, but it had been mostly on her father's land. Never had she done any riding around others because her mother had said she needed to ride with a side saddle if she was going to be seen by people outside her family.

Bert mounted the horse and told her to step on his foot as he reached a hand down to help her up.

She did as she was told and found she needed to hike her skirt up a little and ride astride, keeping her arms tightly around him. She said a silent prayer that no one would see them, and she hung on tight, certain she would fall if she didn't.

Bert was annoyed by how slowly he needed to ride back to the ranch. They were doing their best to get everything ready for winter, but he'd run out of barbed wire, and the cattle didn't like to stay in one place without it. Thankfully, Jim, the store owner had anticipated at least one of the ranchers in the area would have that problem, and he had some in stock.

When they pulled up to the ranch house, Tabitha gaped at it in surprise. It was huge. The man she'd taken for a run of the mill cowboy who slept in a bunkhouse with other men, instead owned a beautiful home and apparently a nice-sized ranch.

He stopped and helped Tabitha down. He wrestled with whether or not to get straight back to work, and have Tabitha introduce herself to Alice, or whether he should go in with her, and finally he decided to do the polite thing and go inside with her.

"I'll introduce you to my housekeeper, and then I'll get back to work."

He strode toward the door, not even offering to carry her carpet bag. Tabitha thought he was the poorest mannered man she'd ever met, but there was nothing much she could do about it.

Once inside the house, he bellowed out, "Alice!"

An older woman—around fifty or so—hurried into the room, wiping her hands on an apron. "Yes, Mr. Blander?"

"Alice Duncan, meet Tabitha Murphy. Tabitha came here to marry someone who did not collect her from the stagecoach, so I'm going to introduce her around at church tomorrow morning. She's staying here until then."

Tabitha turned to thank him for his hospitality, but he was already out the door. "Is he the rudest man alive or am I imagining things?" she asked Mrs. Duncan.

"He's certainly not the politest man I've ever met, and I won't go any further than that." Mrs. Duncan grinned at her. "Let me show you to your bedroom. You'll be upstairs with George and me."

"Thank you so much for helping me. If I can be of any help with supper or anything else, you just let me know."

"Thank you, but I can manage things. I'm sure you're tired after traveling. Would you like me to draw you a bath?"

"I would like that very much. I feel like I have five days of grime covering me, and I'm not sure I'm very far off from that. A bath would make me the happiest woman alive."

"You should set your cap for Bert," Mrs. Duncan said, surprising her. "He had a fiancé who ran off with some idiot, and decided marriage just wasn't for him."

"That's sad. I don't think I could marry such a rude man though. I've already kicked him. Twice."

Mrs. Duncan threw back her head and laughed. "And that's just why you should marry him. He's used to everyone treating him as if he's the king of the valley, but that's very inaccurate. He needs a woman who can stand up to him."

"He probably does, but does he *want* a woman who can stand up to him?"

"Of course, he does. He may not know it yet, but he does." Mrs. Duncan turned to leave the room. "The bathroom is at the end of the hall. I'll start the water."

"You have a bathroom? I've seen them of course, but I never dreamed I would live in a home with one. Of course, I don't live here, but I'm staying here tonight, and I can pretend."

"And you should pretend. Oh, you're going to give old Bert a run for his money."

"Old?" Tabitha asked. Mrs. Duncan was clearly much older than Mr. Blander.

"He's acted like an old man since the day he was born. My husband and I worked for his parents before we worked for him. She died when he was still just sixteen, and his father died when he was twenty-four. He's alone in the world now. Well, we're here with him, but he has no family. He's not the kind of man to really talk about his troubles, so I fear he's living a very lonely life."

"That's sad," Tabitha said, surprised she cared at all that the rude man she'd met was alone. She did though. For whatever reason.

Mrs. Duncan started the bath, and Tabitha watched how it worked, so she could do it herself. "Thank you for all your help," she told Mrs. Duncan.

"After your bath, come downstairs and we'll chat some more. If you don't need a nap that is."

"Not as much as I need to be clean and need to learn about the men around here. I'll be down." Tabitha closed the door to the bathroom and stripped as quickly as she could. The knowledge she would soon be soaking in a tub spurred her on. She was stiff, dirty, and sore, and she hoped a real bath would help all three things.

She got out of the tub an hour later, feeling much cleaner and just a bit wrinkled. She wrapped a towel around herself and hurried into her bedroom, pleased she didn't meet anyone along the way.

Once she was dressed with her hair brushed dry, she went down the stairs into the kitchen. "You look much better!" Mrs. Duncan told her.

"I feel much better," Tabitha agreed. "I wasn't sure I'd be able to force myself to get out, but the water was getting cold."

"I wait to bathe until my husband and Mr. Blander are out for the day, so I can take as long as I like to soak. I've spent countless hours in that bathtub. I think it's my favorite place on God's green earth."

"I don't blame you." Tabitha shook her head. "I did truly enjoy that bath."

Mrs. Duncan looked at Tabitha. "So Mr. Blander is going to introduce you to our bachelors at church tomorrow? What are you looking for in a husband?"

Tabitha shrugged. "I'm looking for a man who has a roof over his head, and I don't want to marry a man who lives in a bunkhouse."

"Well, that disqualifies ninety percent of the men in town. What about appearance?"

"That doesn't matter much to me," Tabitha responded, but as she did, she couldn't stop thinking about the way Mr. Blander's hair had curled around his cowboy hat. Sure, it meant he needed a haircut, but he was a mighty handsome man.

"All right. Do you care what they do for a living?"

Tabitha shook her head. "I expected to marry a man who I would have to work alongside, and I'm still willing to do so."

"There are a few men in town who are starting their own spreads. I'm certain Mr. Blander will introduce you." Mrs. Duncan put the bread pans into the oven and walked over to sit at the table with Tabitha. "You'll have the best life with Mr. Blander. I know he's rude. He's not perfect. But he's a very good man, and he's lonely."

Tabitha bit her lip. "He's not shown any kind of interest in me."

"I'll encourage him to take you for a walk after supper. That'll help things along."

"I'm not certain that's a good idea..."

"I am. You were taught to listen to your elders, right?'

Tabitha's lips quirked into a smile as she nodded. "Yes."

"Well, then listen to me. This is the smartest thing you can possibly do in this situation."

Tabitha was skeptical, but she nodded slowly. "If you say so."

"I do say so. I'll shout it from the rooftops if I have to!"

"Let me help you cook then." Tabitha still wasn't certain she even wanted to give Mr. Blander a chance to get to know her, but she did know she needed to marry someone. Going home to Beckham was not an option.

Chapter Three

When Bert walked into the house that evening for supper, he was still thinking about Tabitha Murphy. Why would a woman be willing to leave behind everything she knew to marry an absolute stranger? It just didn't make any kind of sense to him.

The dining table was set, which surprised him. He usually ate in the kitchen with George and Mrs. Duncan. "Why are we eating in the dining room?" he asked as he washed his hands at the kitchen sink.

Mrs. Duncan poked Bert in the chest, which wasn't a huge surprise. She didn't act like a housekeeper with him. "You're eating in the dining room with your guest. I've spent half the day with her, and I promise you, there is not a woman alive who is better suited to you. You're going to take her for a walk after supper, and you are going to beg her to forgive your rudeness and be your wife. You hear me?"

Bert frowned. Mrs. Duncan had been a second mother to him growing up, and he wasn't about to upset her. He knew she had his best interests in mind. "I don't see how I can do that. I will bring in her chest after supper though."

"Robert Bartholomew Blander, you are a blind man. You can't see that an attractive woman has come from the east to get married. She may be the only woman in the entire state of Wyoming who can stand up to you. Why wouldn't you take the chance to marry her?"

Bert sighed. "You stand up to me quite well," he said, wishing—not for the first time—that she would remember she was the housekeeper and not his mother. "I guess I can walk with her, but don't get your hopes up. She doesn't like me any more than I like her."

Mrs. Duncan shook her head. "And why can't you just be nice to people? You see a girl, sitting on a bench in town, and you make fun of her for coming here to marry a stranger? You should have better manners than that. Your mother and I did our best to pound them into your head."

"But I'm the thickest headed man alive. I know! I know!"

"Well, I'm surprised to hear you admit that," Tabitha said from behind him.

Bert slowly turned. "I'm sorry I was rude. I was taught better. Would you walk with me after supper?"

Tabitha laughed softly. "Are you afraid of your housekeeper, Mr. Blander?"

"Of course, I am. I'm not senile!"

Mrs. Duncan shook her head. "Get to the table, and I'll start serving supper."

Bert did as he was told, noting that Tabitha was following behind him. "Why did you have to get me in trouble?"

"I didn't realize I would! She asked how we met, so I told her. How did I know she was going to treat you like a child?"

He sighed. "She was there for my birth. I've always seen her as more of a second mother than a housekeeper."

Tabitha was surprised at how natural their conversation was after their terrible beginning. "No siblings?"

He shook his head. "No. Ma said she'd always hoped for more, and it just never happened."

"My mother said she took one look at me and never let my father touch her again. She wasn't particularly fond of me, and cheered when I said I was coming west to marry a stranger. She was just never...well...warm and affectionate."

"You should have met my mother. She would have opened her arms and taken you in, wanting you to live with us forever. It's just how she was."

Tabitha smiled. "It sounds like you miss her a lot."

"I do. And my father as well, but he wasn't as warm and affectionate as Ma. He was more the type to work hard for his family and expect everyone else to toe the line."

"I understand. My father was more affectionate than my mother, but they were really both quite distant. I worked for a family back east, and we didn't need the extra money, but Mother didn't want me underfoot all day, so I worked for them."

"What did you do?" he asked, taking a piece of bread, and buttering it.

"I cooked, cleaned, minded their children, ran errands, worked in their garden. Basically I did what I was told for ten hours ever day for twenty cents per day, and my mother was happy to be rid of me."

"Twenty cents per day? Can I hire you to help Mrs. Duncan for that? I promise I wouldn't work you half as hard."

She shook her head. "No, I came here to marry. Mrs. Duncan was telling me about some of the eligible bachelors in town." Though none of them sounded good to her at all. And now that she was looking at Bert again, he didn't look half as quarrelsome.

Bert frowned, a line appearing between his eyebrows. "Is that so?"

Tabitha nodded. "Yes, It's hard to know what I want to do though."

"Mrs. Duncan thinks I should marry you and not let the other men have a chance."

"She told me pretty much the same thing all day long."

He shook his head. "That woman gets something in her head and nothing else will do. Do you know how long I'll hear what an idiot I am if I don't marry you and you marry someone else in town?"

She laughed. "Well, I've decided she's my friend, and if I don't marry you, expect me to be here often, visiting her."

The idea of her being married to someone else and visiting at his place, seeing her expecting someone else's baby...it wasn't something he wanted to think about. "We'll walk after supper and talk. Maybe she's right." He would think she wanted to marry him for his money, but she'd come there planning to work alongside her husband, not to be cared for.

"I'd like that." Now that she was seeing him in a different light, and he wasn't being rude to her constantly, she thought maybe a marriage between them could work. "I won't be the most obedient wife in the world. If that's what you're looking for, you need to forget all about me."

"I used to think it was what I was looking for. Now I'm not so certain."

After supper, he took her for a walk, having her get a shawl so she wouldn't get cold. She hugged it about her shoulders as she walked with him out across the ranch into a grove of trees. "My mother loved applesauce. The year they married, Pa planted these apple trees, so she could always make as much as she wanted. They were Ma's job, though, and she was the one who picked the apples and she and Mrs. Duncan would make the sauce together."

"I bet you have very fond memories of her and her applesauce."

"I do. Do you like applesauce?"

She nodded. "But only with cinnamon." She stumbled over a small hole, and he offered his arm to steady her.

"It's only good with cinnamon," he said, smiling at her. "So you cook?"

"I do. It's the only household chore that I really enjoy, to be honest. I do them all, and will until the day I die, I'm sure, but being in a kitchen makes me happy." She grinned. "My mother hated to cook, so she showed me the basics and it was my job to cook for the family from the time I was nine."

He shook his head. "You don't want to have to go back there, do you?"

"I won't go back there. I'll work here for some money and take the train to the next stop and the next if I have to. I will not go back to my parents' house." She sighed. "I make it sound like life was horrible there, but it wasn't. I just...I'm ready to be married and start having children. I always wanted to have at least a dozen, but I'm getting to the point where I won't be able to have that many if I get much older. I'm already twenty-two!"

"That's not old at all!"

She shrugged. "Everyone back home thought I was much too old to be unmarried."

He stopped walking and turned to her. "May I kiss you?"

She was surprised he asked. He seemed like the type to just grab a woman and kiss her silly. "Why?"

He smiled. "I want to see if we're compatible, and that's the best way to tell."

"And if you don't like kissing me?"

"Then I'll give you the money for a few more train stops, so you can see if you can find a man who will suit you better."

She thought about it for a moment and then nodded. "All right. I'll give that a chance then."

He put his hands on either side of her waist and pulled her toward him. She'd expected a light peck on the lips, but instead, he tucked her body into his, leaned down, and kissed her with a passion she had never imagined. His lips toyed with hers, and his tongue slipped into her mouth.

She hadn't realized a man would use his tongue when kissing, but she liked it, so she stood on tiptoe to get even closer to him, and she bravely moved her tongue into his mouth, which seemed to surprise him.

They stood joined together that way for a long while, his hands moving over her back, caressing every inch of her. When one hand moved down to her backside, she knew she needed to stop him, though she had no desire to do so. She wanted to spend the rest of her life right there in the middle of the apple trees with him.

She removed his hand from where it had roamed and took a step back, her chest heaving. Never in her life had she imagined a kiss could be so...much. It was everything she'd thought about when she'd thought about how babies were made. She knew there was more, but she'd never let herself think about that.

After a moment of just staring at each other in the darkness, she asked, "Are we compatible?"

He smiled. "We're more than compatible. Marry me."

Tabitha stood there with her hand on her mouth that still burned from his kisses. "Yes, I'll marry you."

"We'll have the preacher marry us after church in the morning." He wrapped an arm around her as they walked back toward the house. "I would have Mrs. Duncan stay home from church to move your things down to my room, but I think it would be best if she went with us. Everyone needs to know we slept in different beds for the one night you were here."

"And I need my trunk carried in," she said. "I'll move my own things after we get home tomorrow. There's not much upstairs, and if my trunk is moved into your room, I can get what I need from it tonight, and just leave it down there."

"That sounds wonderful. I hope you know there will be no separate beds."

"I want babies. I couldn't accept separate beds."

The short walk back to the house was spent in silence as she thought about what it would mean to have Bert's hands move over her with no clothing on. One of her married friends had described the entire mating process to her, and although it hadn't sounded pleasant at the time, now it sounded downright exciting.

After the trunk was brought inside the house, Bert excused himself to go and take a bath, while Tabitha and Mrs. Duncan went through her clothes, decided what she'd wear for the wedding, and unpacked most of her things. "Tomorrow should just be a matter of moving a few things down," Tabitha said.

"I'm glad you're marrying my Bert," Mrs. Duncan told her. "I knew the moment I saw you that you needed to marry him."

Tabitha smiled at the older woman. "I feel like I'm doing the best thing. Bert kissed me and my whole body felt like it was on fire."

"Then he's the right man for you. That's how my George made me feel the first time we kissed back in school. He would chase me around at recess, and when he caught me, the kisses came right after. I only ran because I knew he would catch me, and we'd kiss. Oh, I miss those days."

Tabitha laughed. "Well, I'm not sure if I'll be running from Bert or not, but the kisses sure are nice."

"I'm surprised you let him kiss you."

"He told me it was the only way to know if we were truly compatible, and if we weren't after a kiss, then he would give me money to go further west on the train, so I could find someone I did want to marry. It seemed like it would be good for me either way."

"I'd have kissed him too." Mrs. Duncan shook her head. "I'm used to doing everything around the house, so you let me know if you want me to keep doing that, or if I should let you do some of the work as well."

"I love to cook, so I'd love to take that over, if you don't mind. Cook and bake both, actually."

"That sounds nice. I'd be happy to give up those chores."

"Did you make applesauce already?" Tabitha asked.

"He talked to you about his mother's grove of apple trees and her love for apple sauce, didn't he?"

"He did. If you haven't already made it for this year, I'd love to do it with you. I like to add a lot of cinnamon to mine, and it sounds like that's how Bert prefers it as well."

"Oh, it is. I use less than his mother did, but he still likes it."

"Well, perhaps we'll blend my receipt and hers, and we'll have a new type of applesauce we'll all love. I told him I'd take care of the apple trees."

"We'll do it together," Mrs. Duncan said.

"Sounds good to me. I look forward to having you beside me as I navigate newlywed life. Perhaps you can teach me little things I don't know yet."

"I would love to teach you everything I know."

Bert came in then and they left him alone in his room. Tabitha felt odd just being in there with him before they were married, even with Mrs. Duncan there. Oh, marriage to Bert would be wonderful. She just hoped she wouldn't have to kick him very often.

Bert watched her go, still thinking of the kiss they shared. Marrying a woman with the kind of passion Tabitha had was something he'd always dreamed about. And now it was going to happen.

Chapter Four

Bert drove the buggy to church the following morning instead of riding his horse as usual. He couldn't stop sneaking glances at Tabitha, amazed at how much different she looked than when he'd first seen her beside the stagecoach depot.

Her white blouse was such a contrast to her dark hair, and her forest green skirt cinched in at the waist, making him remember how it felt to have his hands on her the night before. He couldn't believe he was marrying a woman who was all but a stranger, but if their kiss the night before was any indication, he had made the right decision.

When they reached town, he caught her by her slim waist and helped her down from the buggy. "I cannot wait until our wedding night," he whispered, his lips all but touching her ear.

She grinned up at him. "I have a feeling I'm going to enjoy it as much as you do."

"I sure hope so. I'm going to try my best to make sure it's an experience neither of us will ever forget."

His arm was around her waist as he guided her into the church. It was both the local school and church, and not exactly what she was used to in the way of a church. Though Tabitha had gone to the country school south of Beckham, they had always made the drive into town for the real church, as her mother had called it. She'd always refused to go to the country church.

Right behind them were George and Alice Duncan, ready to vouch for them that they'd stayed on separate floors of the house the night before. Alice stood with Tabitha and introduced her to different ladies of the church as Bert's fiancée.

Bert had gone to the front of the church to talk to the pastor, asking him to perform the ceremony after church.

When Bert came back to Tabitha, he said, "Pastor Monahan wants to perform the ceremony before our church service. Is that all right with you?"

Tabitha nodded. "Sure." Then she could write to her mother and tell her she'd had the big ceremony her mother had always said her child should have for her wedding. She was only sorry there wasn't a photographer there.

Tabitha waited with Alice, speaking with her in low tones about different things they would be doing that week—like making applesauce.

Bert came to Tabitha a few minutes later, took her hand, and led her to the front of the church, where they stood in front of the pastor, whose voice boomed out over the congregation.

"Dearly Beloved. We're here today to join Bert and...what's your name, child?"

"Tabitha."

"Bert and Tabitha in the rights of holy matrimony. Anyone got anything against them marrying?" When no one spoke up, the pastor continued. "All right, let's get on with it then."

The rest of the ceremony went quickly. They spoke their vows, and then, to Tabitha's surprise, Pastor Monahan said, "Okay, you're husband and wife. Now we want to see a big kiss that tells us this marriage is going to be for real. Kiss her, Bert!"

Tabitha's eyes widened, and she looked at the pastor as if he'd lost his mind. Bert seemed to be expecting it though, and he turned her toward him, moved his arms around her, and he kissed her with the same passion he had the night before.

Even though she knew there was an audience, she reacted to his kiss the same way she had the night before. She went up on her tiptoes to get closer to him, and wrapped her arms around him.

She didn't know how much time passed while they were locked in their embrace, but finally the pastor cleared his throat, reminding them both they had an audience for their passion.

The pastor shook his head. "That was not a church kiss. This is a place of worship!"

Tabitha's face was beet red as they took their seats for the church service. And wouldn't you know? The entire sermon was on wives obeying their husbands. Tabitha knew she would never be a meek and obedient wife, and she tried to think whether she'd told Bert that the night before, but as then, her mind was clouded with passion, and she couldn't remember.

She would just have to tell him on the way home, so she could make sure that he knew. She wasn't going to pretend to be meek and obedient when it wasn't something she believed in at all.

She squirmed in her seat, bumping into Bert repeatedly, not at all comfortable with the sermon. Perhaps it was the right way to do things, but she refused to agree to follow whatever a man told her to do. She didn't know him well enough for one thing. And for another...well, she wasn't feeling obedience when she looked at him. She'd listen to his views, and try to do what he wanted, but if she felt his views were wrong, she wouldn't obey. It was that simple.

Tabitha was thrilled when church was finally over, and she planned to tell Bert exactly what she thought on the drive home. She couldn't wait to get out of the church, but there was a line of people there waiting to meet her. One woman stuck out to her.

"I'm Gladys Sinclair. It's so good to meet you." Gladys was pretty, but very soft-spoken.

"Hi. I'm Tabitha."

"I'm your closest neighbor. I'd love it if you'd come over for tea one day this week. It will be nice to have a neighbor close to my age." Gladys held a child of around three in her arms.

"I'd like that. Maybe late in the week? Alice and I are going to make and can applesauce early this week."

"How about Friday? Bring Alice with you. I adore her."

"All right. We'll be there. What time?"

"Let's say two in the afternoon. That's this one's nap time, and it will be so much easier if she's sleeping."

The little girl took the two fingers she had in her mouth out. "I have tea."

"Maybe tomorrow," Gladys said to her daughter.

"Two sounds fine to me," Tabitha said.

"Wonderful. I'll see you then!" Gladys moved out of the way, and another woman was there, wanting to talk to her.

As they walked out of the church together sometime later, Tabitha said, "I think I met every woman in the entire state of Wyoming. There was a line! What did they all want with me?"

"They wanted to welcome you to the community." He wasn't willing to tell her the truth though. As the wealthiest man in the entire area, people would want to be her friend, hoping for donations to their favorite causes...in some cases, those causes were themselves.

On the drive home, she remembered she needed to talk to him about obedience and marriage.

"I need you to understand that I'm not the type of woman to be blindly obedient to you. I have a mind that I like to use, and I'll listen to your opinions, and I'll make my own decisions. That whole sermon today had me feeling like I was going to be the worst wife alive." She stole a glance in his direction and saw he was laughing.

"What's so funny?" she asked, upset that he wasn't taking her seriously.

"I knew you wouldn't be an obedient wife when you kicked me in town. I can't believe you felt the need to tell me you wouldn't be obedient. I can see that on my own."

"I feel like kicking you again now," she said, frowning at him.

"I'm sure you do, but there's one rule in my buggy. Don't kick the driver!"

"You just made up that rule," she said, glaring now.

"Well, it's a good rule to have. Will you be obedient to the no kicking the driver rule, dear wife?" Bert's lips were still quivering with amusement.

"Yes, it's a rule that makes sense. I wouldn't want you driving off the road or anything. I'll reserve my kicks for when we're not in a moving vehicle." Tabitha hid her grin by looking out the other way, knowing he wouldn't see her face.

"Does that mean that if you get mad at me while I'm driving you won't kick me ever? Or that you won't kick me until the buggy stops?"

"I guess we'll find out, won't we?"

He groaned. "I married a woman who is not sweet, threatens me, and flat out refuses to be obedient. What was I thinking?"

"If the buggy wasn't moving, I'd kiss you and remind you."

He chuckled. "Now that's a threat I hope you'll carry out when we get home."

She laughed, briefly resting her head on his shoulder. "I'll do my best to remember. Sometimes these things just seep out of my brain."

"I need to talk to you about a conversation I had with George this morning. He has asked that he be allowed to use the foreman's cabin as he did when my parents were alive. It wasn't until after Ma died that they moved into the house, so Alice could take care of things easier. But with you there, and willing to do the cooking, she won't need to be there as many hours. Would that bother you?"

She nodded. "I think that's perfect. I like the idea of the house being a little more...private than it would be with them living there. I mean, I know they'll be in and out certain hours, but it'll be better than the way it is now. If I want to sit on your lap in the parlor and kiss you, I wouldn't feel comfortable doing it with Alice and George around."

He smiled. "I like the idea of you sitting on my lap and kissing me. I don't care if it's in the parlor or in the dining room."

"I have a feeling, we're going to enjoy each other a great deal," she said softly. "It will be nice to be alone and know when the Duncans will be around."

His arm wrapped around her, and he kissed her forehead. "I'm sure Alice is making us a nice lunch, but maybe we can say you're making supper after, so they can make themselves scarce."

"Oh, you're not thinking we'll have our wedding night after lunch, are you? It's called a wedding *night* for a reason, I'm sure."

He chuckled. "I'm not sure I can wait until it's actually night. Not if you keep talking about kissing and sitting on my lap..."

"Maybe I can go with Alice to the foreman's cabin and help her get it cleaned up. It must be a mess after years of sitting idle."

He shook his head. "Alice goes up there for a couple hours every week to make sure it's clean, in case we have visitors. Their son brings his family at least once a month or so."

"Oh, that's nice! They'll be happy to have the cabin then."

"It's actually more of a house than a cabin," he said. "There are three bedrooms, a kitchen, and a parlor. What else would someone want?"

"That sounds nice. And your father built that for them?"

He shook his head. "That's the cabin my grandfather built when they first came west on the Oregon Trail. They lived in it until this house was built in 1861."

"That makes sense," she said. "It would take an exceptional man to build a nice house like that for employees."

"My father and grandfather were both exceptional men, but the house was already there. Father hired George and Alice about five years before I was born."

"And they moved in there then?"

He nodded. "They've always seen that as their real home, and they're excited to move back into it."

"Well, I can't say I'm disappointed."

He stopped the buggy in front of the house before walking around to catch her by the waist and lift her down. He held her close and let her slide down the front of his body. "I wish they would leave now," he said softly.

She smiled. "It'll happen soon enough."

"Ten minutes ago isn't soon enough for me."

They walked into the house and saw that their meal was on the dining room table, along with a cake. As soon as they walked in, Alice popped in from the kitchen. "I've done all the dishes except the ones you're about to eat from. Do you want me to stay and do those dishes as well?"

Tabitha smiled. "I think I can do some dishes. It won't hurt me a bit."

"Then I'll be off. There should be enough food there for your supper as well, and I'll be back in the morning to get you anything else you need," Alice promised.

"Perfect. Thank you so much for making the day easy for us."

Bert grinned. "Do you think I could talk George into unhitching the horses and putting them up for the night?"

Alice laughed. "He's working on it now."

Tabitha understood then why the older couple had left church a few minutes early and left her to deal with the line of women alone. They were making their wedding day as private and free from work as they possibly could.

They ate as Alice gathered a few things and left the house. "That was very kind of them to make our day so easy for us." Tabitha cut off a piece of the roast beef.

"And private. Don't forget private."

She smiled. "Oh, I suppose we should pray rather than just eating. I can't believe we almost forgot! We need God in our marriage."

They bowed their heads and he prayed for them, asking God to help them with their marriage and help them to get along together.

As soon as they were finished eating, Tabitha put the food that was left into the ice box and washed the dishes. Bert sat at the kitchen table frowning at her. "That could wait, couldn't it?"

"No, it can't. The food would get caked onto the plates and it would take twice as long later. I'll just get it done now, and we won't have to think about it again." Tabitha enjoyed seeing him so anxious for their first night together...or day it would seem. Maybe there was a chance they would fall in love and not simply enjoy being together. She'd like that a lot.

He sighed, watching her as she worked. "How can I make this faster?" he asked.

"Do you want to wipe the dishes dry and put them away?" she asked.

"No."

"Then just sit there. It'll only take a minute or two."

"Fine..."

Chapter Five

As soon as Tabitha put the last plate away, Bert was on his feet. He took her hand and pulled her toward the bedroom. "Let me at least get my apron off," she protested.

He paused long enough for her to take it off and toss it to the table before resuming their short walk to the bedroom. He shut the door behind them, just in case the Duncans had forgotten something.

As soon as the door was closed, he pulled her to him and kissed her until she was unsteady on her feet. When one of his hands cupped her breast, she moaned softly, enjoying his touch.

"All right, turn around, and we'll get this thing off you."

Her blouse buttoned in the back, and he immediately began liberating each button from its hole. He frowned at the corset he discovered. "You don't have to wear this contraption for me," he said.

"My corset?" she asked.

"Yes. They don't seem like they're healthful for women."

She shrugged. "I haven't left my house without one for many years."

"That's fair. Wear one when you go out, but not at home. It just doesn't seem like it would be good for you."

"My mother always told me I'd get so thick no man would ever look at me if I didn't wear one all the time. So I wear one."

"But no more, right?"

She turned in his arms, not thinking about the fact that her blouse was gone, and she'd be standing there in just her skirt and corset with her breasts pushed up by the garment. "Is it that important to you?" she asked.

He nodded. "I've just never had a use for them. They don't look at all comfortable."

"They don't feel comfortable either," she said. "All right. I'll only wear one when I leave the house."

"Thank you," he said, leaning down and licking the soft flesh that was pushed up by her corset. "Now turn back around, so I can get this thing off you."

He made short work of her corset, making her think he'd dealt with many in the past. "Do you have experience with corsets?" she asked.

"Of course not," he said, but she had no idea if he was telling the truth or not. Didn't most men have experience with women before they married? When her corset was gone, she wore her petticoat beneath it. "How many layers of clothes do you have on?"

"As many as it takes to be modest. Stop complaining. You want a modest wife, don't you?"

"Not particularly. I mean, I don't want you giving a show to all the men in town, but you're my wife. I want you naked as much as possible."

"I'm not going to run around the house naked. I need to be wearing at least an apron."

He chuckled. "I think Alice would have a heart attack if she saw you that way."

"Maybe..."

He unfastened her skirt and pushed it down, then pulled her petticoat off. At last she stood naked before him, other than her knickers, which he happily pushed off for her. "You're beautiful, wife."

"You're clothed, husband." She went to work on his tie, and then unbuttoned his shirt. He took so long to undress her it felt as if hours had passed, and though she knew that wasn't true, she wanted him undressed faster than he seemed capable of doing things.

As soon as his shirt was off, she moved to the buttons on his pants. She was as ready to have him undressed as he was to have her naked. Some of it was that she was aching to find out what making love was like, but also she was curious as to what he looked like without his clothes. She'd seen naked babies—more than her share after working for the Matthews for four years—but she'd never seen a man naked. Once she'd seen a painting that was a statue of a man, but her mother had covered her eyes. She hadn't had time to really study him *there*.

And while she knew the basics of lovemaking, she had no idea what it would actually be like and feel like. And her curiosity was about to get the better of her. She'd tried to ask her mother a couple of questions before leaving, but her mother had told her the best way to learn was to submit to her husband and allow him his rights. That hadn't helped at all.

When he was completely naked, she took a step back to gaze at him. Her eyes locked onto his member, and she stared at it for a moment, finally stating what she thought was completely obvious. "Baby boys are much smaller there."

He chuckled. "They grow as a boy grows up."

"I see that. Is it soft?"

"You're welcome to touch it and see for yourself."

Tabitha didn't need another invitation. She reached out and touched him with one finger. "Oh, it's soft. Feels like velvet." She stroked it with her whole hand. "It's hard underneath the velvet though. Very strange."

He caught her hand and took it off him. "If you keep doing that, we're never going to be able to finish what we started."

She didn't understand that, but it was fine. Instead, she floated into his arms and wrapped her own arms around him. "Show me."

Bert didn't have to be asked twice. Or told twice as the case may be.

He lifted her and laid her on one side of the bed. In a moment, he was in beside her, and his hands were stroking her everywhere. When one hand went between her thighs and stroked the secret flesh nestled there, she gasped and caught his wrist. That felt too good for it to be all right. "You shouldn't do that!"

"Why not?" he asked.

"It…It feels good. Really good. That can't be all right." Wasn't there something in the Bible that said if it feels good, don't do it? She knew it was there somewhere.

"It's fine. I promise. It feels just as good to me when you touch me."

"But…Are you sure that's all right?"

He stroked her again, causing her to arch into his hand. "Positive." He covered her lips with his own so she couldn't protest anymore, not that her protests were real. She was obviously enjoying herself more than expected.

A short while later, they lay beside each other on the bed, each of them breathing heavily. "Can we do that every day?" she finally asked.

"We will do that as often as possible." He pulled her to him and held her tightly. "You really enjoyed it, didn't you?"

"Yes. My whole body aches from it, but…wow. I didn't expect to see a rainbow."

He chuckled. "A rainbow?"

"Everything turned into a rainbow at the end. It was the most glorious experience of my life."

"Then we'll do it often."

"And it's okay that I liked it so much?"

"Yes, it's very okay that you liked it. I think I liked it more than you did." As Bert spoke, his hands moved over her continually. He couldn't believe the feisty woman beside him was really his wife. She was perfect in every way.

She leaned over him, kissing him. "So how shall we spend the rest of the day?"

He chuckled. "Well, I don't know. I usually read the paper after church on Sundays. If you enjoy reading, many of my mother's books are on the shelf in the parlor."

Her eyes widened. "You wouldn't think I was frittering my time away if I read something?"

"Of course not. It doesn't matter what you read. It's all good for your mind."

"Then I will happily read a book while you read the paper." She'd been taught that reading when you could be doing something more productive was bad for the mind. Not by a teacher of course, but by her mother.

She jumped out of bed and pulled a nightgown over her head. "There's no point in dressing if we're not leaving the house today," she announced.

"Maybe not," he said.

He pulled an old pair of faded Levis on and left his shirt off. Why dress if she wasn't going to?

In the parlor, he showed her which books had been his mother's and she chose one she'd heard about but never read. She'd sneaked and read her teacher's copy of *Little Women* by Louisa May Alcott at school during recess, but she'd never been allowed to read *Little Men*. Now she had the chance.

She sat down on the couch, tucking her feet under her to one side, and she lost herself in the book. She was delighted to discover the characters had some carryovers from *Little Women*.

She didn't notice when Bert stood up to turn on the light. She didn't even noticed when he put the paper down and watched her for a few minutes. Finally, she noticed when he asked, "Are you getting hungry?"

She looked at the book, and she realized she'd read the first two hundred pages. No wonder her mother didn't think she should read books. She spent all day and didn't notice time passing around her.

"I'll reheat supper. Sorry, I completely forgot that the world was going on without us."

"What book are you reading?" he asked. When she told him, he smiled. "That was a favorite of mine. *Little Women* was good, but I really preferred *Little Men*."

He followed her into the kitchen and watched as she put supper on the table. "Do you mind eating in here?" she asked. "I can put everything on the table in the dining room as well, but the kitchen seems so cozy."

"No, this is fine. I always ate in the kitchen with the Duncans. I don't know why she set the dining table yesterday."

"Because she was hoping you'd marry me," Tabitha told him. "That's why she had you take me for a walk after supper as well. She was hoping that you'd spend a little time with me and realize that we were meant to be together. She asked me to agree and have an open mind."

He nodded, smiling. "I should have known. She was really excited about me marrying you."

"She told me there's no one else in the area that you would consider, and she was ready for you to settle down and be happy."

"I don't know if I can say that the way you make me feel calms me at all. Or settles me." He reached for her hand as he said a prayer over their food. "I think all you do is get me excited."

She smiled. "Just as you get me excited." She brushed his barefoot with her own under the table.

"You need to stop that if you want to make it through supper," he said, taking a bite of the warmed food. Thankfully, it was just as delicious the second time.

She giggled. "We're going to make and can applesauce this week."

"I'd love that," he said. "I will look forward to having applesauce again. I ate too much of it when I had the flu last winter, and we've been out for a good long while."

"The store in town doesn't have applesauce?" she asked.

"Well, they do, but it certainly doesn't taste like my mother's. To be fair, neither did Alice's, but hers is still good."

"We're going to combine my receipt with your mother's. It should be delicious."

"I can't believe you're going to change my mother's receipt! If it's not as good, I'm going to have something to say about it."

"I'll make sure it's still delicious."

Bert studied her. "If it's not as good, will you make one kind for me and one kind for you?"

"If it's not as good, we will. But I want you to give it a real try, and not just say it's not good enough."

"I will. I wouldn't want to upset my wife now, would I?"

"Probably not," Tabitha said. "I think you want to keep me happy."

"If only to avoid getting kicked again!"

"Why did the pastor tell us to kiss the way we did, and then scold us for doing it?"

Bert shook his head. "He always tells couples to do that, and then everyone laughs when the couple is too embarrassed. I think he expected the same from us, but we didn't get embarrassed."

"I was a little embarrassed," Tabitha told him. "I enjoy kissing you, but with that many people watching, it wasn't as wonderful as it could have been."

"I agree. I should have told everyone to turn away and then kissed you that way."

"Or you could have saved kissing me that way for when we got home."

Bert grinned. "What fun would that have been?"

She shook her head. "Do you have chores to do tonight?"

"Usually, but George and Alice are taking care of them tonight. To give us a little more time together before we have to get back to work tomorrow."

"I suppose that makes sense. I just really want to spend time with you while we can."

"Without kicking me?"

"I'll only kick you when you deserve it, so maybe you should be careful to behave yourself."

He chuckled. "We have a late litter of kittens in the barn. Do you want to see them tomorrow evening?"

She nodded. "Do you like cats?"

He shrugged. "I can take them or leave them. It's good to have a few barn cats to make sure there are no mice, but other than that, I have no idea. I've never had a house cat."

"How old are the kittens?" she asked.

"Five or six weeks, I think. They're eating table scraps now, just like their mama."

"So, they're old enough to be taken from her. How would you feel if we turned one into a house cat? My friend had one when we were little, and I loved it so much. When she had kittens, I begged my mother for one, but she always said no."

"So, this is a lifelong dream of yours to have kittens, I guess?"

"It is."

He sighed. "I'm only letting you have one as a wedding gift. And you're taking care of it on your own."

She jumped up from her chair and hurried to him, hugging him from behind. He pushed out his chair, and pulled her down on his lap, kissing her. "Thank you," she said when he let her come up for air.

"Get these dishes done quickly and thank me properly," he told her.

She giggled and got up and did as she was told. She could be obedient when she agreed with what he wanted. It was other times that were more difficult.

He watched her fly around the kitchen and smiled. "I guess you can be obedient when you want to be."

The kick he received was earned, and he knew it, so he didn't say a thing.

Chapter Six

Before getting up the following morning, Tabitha heard Alice in the kitchen starting breakfast. She knew she should get up and remind the older woman she was going to be the one cooking, but she just wasn't ready to roll out of bed yet.

Instead, she rolled close to Bert and sighed contentedly. Marriage was something she'd always dreamed about, but her first day of being married to Bert had surpassed all expectations and dreams. He was gentle with her, and he seemed to genuinely care about her. What more could a bride ask for?

Bert woke slowly, his hand stroking her hair. "Is it morning already?" he asked.

"Alice is in the kitchen cooking breakfast, so I have to assume it is indeed morning."

He sighed. "Come out with me to do the chores, and you can meet the kittens."

"I would love that! If I fall in love with one of them, may I bring it inside today?"

"Sure," he said. He still wasn't certain about having a cat inside the house, but if it made her as happy as it seemed to, he was more than willing. He needed her to stay happy so they could continue to have days like they'd just had. He'd never dreamed he'd find a wife who was so willing in bed. His former fiancé had been afraid for him to even kiss her.

They both dressed quickly, and she went to the kitchen to tell Alice what they were doing. "I appreciate you getting breakfast on the table this morning."

Alice smiled. "I thought it might help you if I did breakfast every morning. That way you don't have to wake early, but you can cook the other meals, which should give you enough cooking to do to keep you happy."

Tabitha hugged the older woman. "Thank you! I'm off to look at the kittens in the barn now."

"Oh, will you be choosing one for the house?" Alice asked.

"Yes, I will."

"I'll start work on a cat bed later today then. Are we still planning to work on applesauce today?"

"Yes, we are. I cannot wait until Bert tries my applesauce. I want to just make mine today, and if he doesn't like it, we'll use his mother's receipt tomorrow."

Alice nodded. "We'll do that then."

Tabitha met up with Bert at the front door, keeping her shawl tightly around her shoulders. "It's chilly."

"We'll have snow any day," he told her. "Better get used to cold, because ours lasts months at a time."

"Oh, that's awesome. I can't wait!"

He laughed softly. "You're so happy about everything I tell you about living here. I hope you'll still be happy after nine months of winter."

"Why not? I enjoy cold weather."

They walked out to the barn together, where they saw George milking one of the cows. "I was coming out to do that!" Bert said to George.

George shrugged. "I thought it would be nice if I took over the morning milking. Gives you time to sleep a little later."

Bert grinned. The older man was going to give him a chance to be with his wife in the mornings. How kind.

"Thank you. I appreciate it! Tabitha and I are here to see the kittens."

"They're over in the corner where their mama keeps them."

Bert led Tabitha to the corner, and there were four kittens wrestling and playing there. Tabitha sank to the floor, where she sat with her legs crossed, watching the kittens. One was pure black, one was pure white, and the other two were a mix of the two colors. She watched them until one of the black and white kittens plopped down on her lap and nudged her head against Tabitha's hand.

Tabitha immediately scratched her ears, and the kitten purred against her hand. "This is the one," she said to Bert, who had been standing over her watching the kittens.

"All right," he said. He took the kitten and turned it over. "It's a girl. What are you going to name her?"

Tabitha frowned. "I don't know. I'll watch her personality and come up with something that suits her."

She got to her feet and took the kitten back from him, cradling it against her chest. "Let's get you inside, and we'll get you some warm milk. Or maybe some eggs for breakfast."

"You're going to spoil that kitten, aren't you?"

Tabitha grinned at Bert. "Of course I am!"

Together they moved back toward the house, with Tabitha carrying the kitten. Once inside, she went straight to the kitchen with her new friend, setting her on the floor. Alice had already warmed milk, and she put it in a bowl, and then put a bowl of it on the floor for the little one.

The baby licked it excitedly.

Tabitha watched it as it licked at the milk, glad it wasn't making a huge mess, which is what she'd half expected. "Do you think you could make an egg or two for her as well?" she asked, not even looking at Alice.

"Oh, of course. I made eggs, bacon, and toast for you and Bert."

"Sounds good to me," Tabitha said, unable to take her eyes off the little ball of fluff.

"The food is on the table in the dining room whenever you're ready for it."

"That means now," Bert said from behind her. "Thank you, Alice."

"Of course. And I'll keep an eye on the little critter while you eat. Does it have a name yet?" Alice asked.

"She doesn't," Tabitha said. "Now if she were a tabby cat, I'd name her after myself, and we could all call her Tabby. But she's not so we'll have to think of something. I kind of want to get to know her little personality first."

The kitten looked up at Tabitha, its whole face covered in milk. She giggled, but she followed Bert to the dining room.

As they ate their breakfast, she felt the kitten playing under her skirt. She giggled more than once during breakfast, and Bert simply kept smiling at her. "Well, I'm glad we had kittens when you arrived," he finally said.

"Oh, me too. It's nice to have something so small and snuggly that belongs to me."

"Hopefully our babies will be small and snuggly as well," he said.

"Hopefully our babies will be numerous."

They were halfway through their meal when Alice came into the room and set a small dish of eggs on the floor. The kitten walked to them, reached out and touched them with one of her front paws, and then took a small bite. She must have liked it because she made little growling sounds in her throat as she gobbled them up happily.

"What are you doing today?" she finally asked.

"We're moving the cattle closer to the barn. It'll be easier to keep track of them and keep them fed if they're not out on the far reaches of the property."

"That makes sense. Do you keep them close all winter?"

"We try to. Oftentimes, they get out and get stuck in the snow. We'll be working on keeping them in place the whole winter. I want to get a permanent winter enclosure for them, but I'm not sure it'll be done before spring. You'll love spring here," he told her, smiling.

"Why's that?"

"Tons of calves. Some will need to be bottle fed, though usually only one or two per year. Their mothers will die, or they'll reject them."

"Oh, that's sad. Why would a mother reject her baby?" she asked, feeling as if she had something very much in common with the calves that were rejected. She'd always love them the most.

"Usually only the first time mamas do that. They're not really sure what to do with the calf. If I can't get it to start cleaning the calf, I put grain on the calf's back, and usually that will kick in their motherly instinct. If not, I'll bottle feed."

"I'd love to help with the bottle feeding if it needs done this spring."

"If you still feel that way in the spring, I'd be happy for the help. Usually that's left to me or George, and sometimes Alice, depending on how many we have. Sometimes it takes multiple hands to get the work done. My cowboys, who live in the bunkhouse, don't usually mess with the orphan calves."

"I'm going to learn a lot more about ranching in the next few months, won't I? My father has always been a farmer, but he grows crops. We've only had a cow for our own milk over the years."

"You don't talk about your father much. What's he like?" Bert asked.

Tabitha smiled. "When my mother's not around, he's absolutely wonderful. He would sneak away from her to drive me to school on very cold days. We would take walks together, and he would pick flowers for me. When Mother was around, he had to act like she was the most important thing in his entire world though. So he usually mostly ignored me when she was there."

Bert frowned. "Why couldn't he treat you both as if you were important?"

"It would make my mother angry."

"I don't think I understand your parents."

After breakfast, he brushed a quick kiss across her lips. "Have a good day. I'll eat lunch with my men, so I won't see you until supper time."

"Plan on having applesauce for dessert," she said, even though she was thinking of making an apple cake as well. Hopefully he'd enjoy being surprised. It was a little startling how little she knew about him yet.

The kitten followed her when she went into the kitchen with Alice. "Are we ready to get the dishes done, so we can start on applesauce?" she asked.

Alice smiled. "Fall has always been my favorite time of year. I love harvesting a garden and canning everything I harvest. It just brings a bit of joy to my life."

"I will be working by your side. I kept up a kitchen garden for the people I worked for back east, and then it was my job to can everything. It was hard, though, because there were so many children to mind as I was doing it."

"What about the woman you worked for? Didn't she help?"

"Not if I was there. She figured she needed to get every penny of work out of me she could." Tabitha looked around. "Where can I find the jars for canning?"

"They're in the cellar."

"Oh, I didn't even know we had a cellar. Show me where, and I'll go get some."

Alice smiled. "You're definitely going to be doing your share of work around here, aren't you?"

"If I'm able to, I will always do my share and more." She found the trap door for the cellar, and went down. Thankfully, the cellar had a few windows, and it wasn't difficult to find what she was looking for. There was a burlap sack down there, and she filled it with the jars, knowing she would need to be careful to get them all upstairs without breaking them.

While she scrubbed out the jars, Alice worked on peeling and coring the apples she'd saved for applesauce, and then they switched places after a while and Tabitha peeled while Alice scrubbed the jars. They worked easily together and talked about nothing and everything.

As they worked, the kitten went from running a mile per minute and exploring everything to sleeping on the floor beside Tabitha's foot. "As soon as the applesauce is done, I'm making her a little pillow to sleep on," Tabitha said, looking down at the sweet kitten.

"Have you come up with a name for her yet?" Alice asked, eyeing the rambunctious kitten with trepidation. "She definitely enjoys being in the house with us. Will you let her out at times?"

"Oh, of course. I want her to get used to being inside first."

"She's a roly poly little thing, isn't she?"

"Oooo. I could call her Polly. Cuz she's a roly-Polly."

Alice smiled. "I like that."

"I do too! All right, Polly it is."

The kitten woke then, arching her back in a stretch, before spinning around and settling back down. "I think she likes her name," Alice said.

"I think so too."

By the end of the evening, they had forty jars of applesauce ready, and there was some left for supper that evening. "Do you think Bert would like an apple cake for supper?" Tabitha asked.

"Not just apple cake?" Alice asked.

"Oh, no. I'll make some ham and potatoes for supper, and the cake will be dessert."

"Now that sounds like it would be appealing to him. I do have a ham ready to cook in the ice box. I meant to make it for Sunday dinner, but the two of you went and got married, and it slipped my mind."

Tabitha grinned. "Then that's what I'll make. Ham, mashed potatoes, carrots, and apple cake for dessert."

Alice smiled and nodded. "He'll like that. But make twice what you think you'll need."

"Why?" Tabitha asked.

"Because he's going to eat that much after a long day working with the men. And he'd never admit this, but he doesn't much like the bunk house cook's food. So he's always hungry when he works all day and doesn't come in for a lunch break."

"All right. I'll make lots of food."

Alice nodded. "Do you want help with supper?"

Tabitha glanced at the time. It was already five, and Tabitha knew Alice would need to be getting supper on her own table. "Not at all. I've got it."

"All right. I'll see you in the morning then. Remember, George and I will take care of breakfast and morning chores."

"We really appreciate that. I've never been much of a morning person," Tabitha said.

"Neither has Bert, but he won't admit it." Alice left then, off to go cook for her husband and herself.

Tabitha put the ham in the oven and then mixed up the ingredients for the cake. While the cake was baking, she peeled the potatoes, and got a jar of carrots from the cellar. Then she put the potatoes on the stove and found a small pot to heat up the carrots. They hadn't taken the time to bake bread that day, so Tabitha hoped Bert would be all right with just what she'd made.

It was her first real meal to fix for him, so she wanted it to go well, and she wanted him to love her cooking. Hopefully, he would, but knowing Bert, he would let her know either way. He wasn't a man to hide his feelings.

Chapter Seven

After supper—which Bert raved about—they retired to the parlor for a while. He had a new newspaper in his hands, and Tabitha worked on sewing a pillow for little Polly, who played in and out of her skirts. At one point she climbed onto a table, laid on her back, and watched Tabitha sewing. She laid like that for a good long while.

"You are so silly!" Tabitha said, looking at her upside down.

Bert peeked out from behind his newspaper and grinned. "I see you chose the most entertaining kitten of the bunch."

"She chose me," she said, thankful to have a kitten in her life. She'd already laughed more that day watching the antics of Polly than she had in any day of her memory.

Tabitha worked more quickly on the pillow, wanting the kitten to be able to sleep on it. If it was just her, she'd have let the kitten sleep with her, but she had a feeling Bert wouldn't like that very much.

She tied off the last of the thread and put it on the floor, just as Bert put down his paper. "Are you ready for bed?" he asked.

She nodded. "And more than that, Polly is ready for bed." She'd made a pink pillow with leftover fabric she'd found and made it flat and long. That way the kitten would be able to sleep on it when she was older as well.

She removed Polly from the table and put her on the pillow, smiling as the kitten sniffed it and then moved to lay down on the rug. "I guess she doesn't like it," Tabitha said with a frown.

"Give her time to get used to it," Bert told her. "She'll like it more as she is more familiar with it." He reached his hand out to take hers and lead her to bed. "Let's sleep."

She chuckled, raising an eyebrow. "Sleep?" she asked. "Is that really what you're planning to do?"

He pulled her to him and kissed her. "Eventually."

"I like the way you think."

ON FRIDAY, RIGHT AFTER lunch, Tabitha got ready for tea. She had no idea if she should dress up for it or if she should wear her day dress. She sought out Alice who was washing dishes in the kitchen. "Should I dress for tea with Mrs. Sinclair?"

Alice nodded. "I would. Gladys was supposed to marry Bert, but she was scared of him, and ended up marrying Charles Sinclair instead. Charles is very soft-spoken and kind. He suits Gladys well, but Bert would rather you dressed to spend time with her, I think."

"I didn't know they were affianced." Tabitha frowned. "I'll wear my nicest dress that I didn't wear to get married in. Should I take anything?"

"Oh, there's no need for that. Gladys is very sweet, and I'm not surprised she reached out to you right away."

"Well, I think I'm excited to get to know her then."

"Trust me, she has no lasting designs on Bert. In fact, they were still engaged when she married. It was funny how afraid she was every time she was around him. I told him over and over that she wasn't a suitable wife for him, but he simply wouldn't listen."

Tabitha nodded. "All right. Thank you for that information, and now I'll go dress, and you can tell me if I look good enough."

Alice laughed. "You're beautiful, Tabitha. Of course, you'll look good enough."

Tabitha almost wished she didn't know about Gladys being engaged to Bert as she dressed. How was one supposed to react toward the woman who had once broken her husband's heart?

When Tabitha was ready, wearing a blue gingham dress which brought out her blue eyes, she stepped into the kitchen for Alice to see. Alice was making supper that night as well, as Tabitha would be gone for a while.

Alice turned around to look at her, and she smiled, nodding her approval. "You look wonderful. That dress really brings out the blue in your eyes. I do think your eyes are very striking when contrasted with your hair."

Tabitha smiled. It was something she'd heard her entire life. "Thank you." She took a deep breath and saw it was quarter til two. "Are you sure you don't want to come with me?"

Alice shook her head. "I don't think that would be wise." She went to the door and pointed off in the distance. "Her house is just over that hill."

"All right. Wish me luck!"

"I would if you needed it," Alice said.

Polly started to follow Tabitha out of the house, but Alice blocked her with her foot. "Sorry, baby, but you're staying with me." Alice picked up the kitten and snuggled her under her chin.

Tabitha enjoyed the walk to the Sinclairs' house. It was getting chilly, so she wore her shawl, but not so cold it was unpleasant. Bert had assured her it soon would be unpleasant, but there hadn't been any snow yet. Certainly there would be soon.

At the top of the hill, she spotted the house, and was able to walk straight to it. There was a path down the mountain that she was sure had been walked many times.

At the house, she could see a plowed over garden and there was a pretty front porch with a swing for two. It looked like a very cozy home. She raised her hand and knocked at the door.

Gladys came to the door with a smile on her face. "Perfect timing. I just put Melanie down for her nap."

"She's a beautiful child," Tabitha told her. It seemed it was an easy topic. "I tried to talk Alice into coming with me but she said she would stay behind to make supper."

"Alice certainly does have a mind of her own. Come in! The tea is on, and I made cookies for us to snack on."

"Sounds wonderful." Tabitha took a step inside the pristine home. "Do you have a housekeeper? Your home is immaculate!"

"I don't," Gladys said. "I guess I obsess over housework a little more than most women. I like it to always be perfect in case someone stops by."

Tabitha liked to keep a clean home, but she had other things to do as well. "I brought you a jar of applesauce. Alice and I made it on Monday."

"Oh, thank you! I know how much Bert loves his applesauce. You used his mother's receipt, I guess?"

Tabitha shook her head. "Actually, I used my own. He said he liked it better."

"You must be an outstanding cook then. Perhaps I'll have you give me tips. My Charles is always happy with how the house looks, but I think he'd like it if my cooking was a little better. At least I'm no longer burning everything as I did when we were first married."

"How long have you been married?" Tabitha asked. She wanted to ask about her time with Bert, but it would be better if Gladys shared that on her own.

"Five years," Gladys said. "I was supposed to marry Bert, you know."

"Really?" Tabitha asked, acting as if it was new information. "What made you marry Charles instead?"

Gladys sighed as she poured the tea. "My father arranged the marriage with Bert. He never really talked to me about it, but he came home from working on the farm one day, and he told me I was marrying Bert."

"Oh, that would have made me angry."

"It didn't make me angry," Gladys said, sitting down at the table and taking one of the cookies for herself. "It made me scared. There's just something about Bert that was always unnerving to me. He'd kiss me, and I'd want to run away screaming."

Tabitha smiled. "That is not my reaction to his kisses."

"I should hope not! Anyway, I met Charles on a walk one night. He never was religious, and he doesn't go to church and never has. He's about ten years older than me, and he's a farmer, like my father. We talked and walked, and there was just something about him. It was only about a month before I was supposed to marry Bert when Charles asked me to marry him. I hadn't told him about Bert, you see."

"Oh, that must have been a surprise to Charles!"

"I explained the situation, and then I said yes, I'd marry him. But we'd have to do it right away."

Tabitha's eyes widened. "You didn't break it off with Bert first, did you?"

"I was much too afraid of him to break off our engagement. I went home, and I begged my father to break it off, as he was the one who accepted the offer of marriage for me in the first place. He refused. He wanted me to marry Bert because he grew corn. He thought if I was married to Bert, Bert would feel the need to buy his corn for winter feed for his cattle." She shook her head. "So I talked to Charles, and we married the next day. My father hasn't spoken to me since."

Tabitha understood then. Gladys would have been miserable married to Bert. "Do you know the secret to keeping Bert from getting too bossy?" she asked.

Gladys shook her head. "Kick him. I kicked him within five minutes of meeting him. Twice."

Gladys giggled. "I wouldn't have dared do such a thing."

"I have threatened it again, but I don't believe I've kicked him again. He just brings it out in me."

"I cannot imagine he's pleased when you kick him. You're really not afraid of him, are you?"

Tabitha laughed. "I'm a little afraid of what he makes me feel. It's a good thing we're married because I would have been willing to do anything with him after that first kiss."

"I much prefer the softer touch I get from Charles. There's no great passion between us, but he doesn't frighten me either."

Tabitha thought of the passion between her and Bert and smiled. "I don't think we should be discussing our passion for our husbands, should we?" She understood that Gladys would have been a terrible wife for Bert, and that she was the women he was meant to marry. If this visit told her nothing else, she would do well to remember that.

"I just wanted you to understand what happened between Bert and I so you would know I wasn't a threat to you and your marriage."

"Thank you for that. Your cookies are delicious," Tabitha lied. The other woman really did need help in the cooking department.

"Thanks for lying," Gladys said with a grin. "So where did you come from?"

Tabitha explained briefly what had led her to coming west to be a mail-order bride. "I'm just thankful that Bert let me spend that first night I was here. And that Alice convinced us both we belonged together."

"Alice was always telling me that we shouldn't be together. How odd."

"I think we'll both agree I'm better suited to Bert," Tabitha said with a grin.

"Oh, for certain."

"Tell me about your little girl."

Gladys's face lit up at the mention of her baby. "She's three and a half. She's so smart. She knows all her colors, and she can count to ten."

"Oh, that's wonderful."

"You'll have to come back some day when she's awake."

"You should bring her to my place to see my new kitten, Polly."

"Is she a barn cat?" Gladys asked. "I know Bert doesn't think animals should live in houses with people."

"No, she's a housecat. Bert let me choose between the kittens his barn cat had birthed, and Polly walked over and sat on my lap. I'm excited to have her."

"You are seeing a very different side of Bert than I ever did, but it sounds like he makes you happy."

Tabitha nodded. "He does. We have a great deal in common and enjoy spending time together."

"I'm happy for both of you, but especially for Bert. His personality...it's a bit overwhelming at times. I'm just glad he found a match for it."

"Me too."

Tabitha was still thinking about all Gladys had said as she walked back home. It was odd that two women could see the same man and one find him incredibly appealing and the other find him frightening. Tabitha was certain she would find Charles a boring man. Maybe she would meet him one day.

Alice had made a pot roast, mashed potatoes, and carrots for supper. They'd made several loaves of bread that morning so Tabitha was certain it would feel like a feast.

After Alice left, but before Bert returned home, Tabitha cut off a small piece of meat and put it into the kitten's bowl. Polly made growling sounds until Tabitha walked away, leaving the kitten to her meal.

Tabitha had just finished setting the table when Bert came into the house at the end of his day. "That smells good. I'm hungry!"

"Alice cooked for us tonight. I was at Gladys Sinclair's having tea with her."

He nodded. "Did you have a nice time?"

"We did. She wanted to assure me she had no desire to get between us in any way."

He frowned at that. "Why would she? She hated being engaged to me."

"No, she was just afraid of you," Tabitha said.

"Why would she be afraid of me?" he asked. "That woman never did make any kind of sense."

"She seems like she's afraid of a lot of things. But she's kind, and I feel like she could be a real friend, if that doesn't bother you."

Bert shook his head. "I won't dictate who your friends are. I have no harsh feelings for Gladys. I'm just glad she called it off when she did. There was no way I was going to be able to go through with the wedding."

"Why not?" she asked.

"Every time I tried to kiss her, she'd turn her head away. If I managed to kiss her, she'd start crying. Can you imagine having a wedding night with her?"

"Well, I can't imagine a wedding night with any woman. Or any man but you. I kind of liked our wedding night, though."

He smiled. "I thought it was pretty wonderful myself. In fact, if you're up for it, I'd be happy to have another wedding night tonight."

She laughed at that. "I'm game if you are." Tabitha couldn't help but be thankful for the passion between them. She couldn't imagine what it would be like to be in a marriage like the Sinclairs'. With no passion, what was the sense in being married?

Oh, she knew it wouldn't always be that way between them. But she would keep their passion alive for as long as she could. She enjoyed it too much to do otherwise.

Chapter Eight

As they drove into town for church on Sunday, Tabitha was thinking about the man she'd come to Wyoming to marry. She had yet to meet him, though he'd paid for her train fare, and she'd corresponded with him.

"I wonder why Jacob Small paid for me to come west and then never showed up to meet me at the stagecoach."

Bert shook his head. "As far as I know, the man can't read. He's rarely sober. Maybe someone decided to play a trick on him? But that would be one mighty expensive trick. There aren't too many in this area who could afford to just spend that kind of money for a joke."

"I just...it bothers me. I feel like I should have had some loyalty to him, but I sure do prefer your touch to an insane man's. At least I think I would. You were the first man to kiss me after all."

"All other men should be jealous then."

She bumped him with her shoulder. "I am glad I married you and not someone else."

"Is that so? Does that mean you'll promise to never kick me again?"

"But that's why you wanted to marry me. Because I kicked you."

Bert looked at her. "How did you ever guess?"

"It was obvious. Is there anyone Jacob is close to?"

Bert shrugged. "Still thinking about him, are you? He rarely even goes into town. I've met him only once or twice. Once he was driving his cattle through town. I'm not sure what he was really driving, but I sure didn't see no cattle."

"Maybe you could drive me down near where he lives after church."

Bert sighed. "Will you stop worrying about him if I do?"

"I can't make a promise about that, but I'll feel better about myself. Besides, you should be taking me on romantic drives all the time!"

He shook his head. "I work all the time. Romantic drives are for men who don't know how to work."

"We both know that's not true," she said. "I work hard while you're off working, and I can make time for a romantic drive."

He groaned. "I'll take you for a romantic drive to see the man you were supposed to marry after lunch. I'm eating first."

She put her hand flat against his stomach. "I would never ask you to go hungry!"

"You keep touching me like that, and we're turning around, going home, and missing out on church."

"We have to worship God to thank him for making us the way he did. It's so much fun to procreate!"

He laughed. "It certainly is. We'll have more fun with that later."

When they reached the church, she went in, feeling a little more confident about facing all the strangers in the church. She wasn't as shy as Gladys, but she didn't like to face a large crowd of people she didn't know, either.

Immediately, Bert went off to talk with a group of men dressed similarly to himself. Tabitha assumed they were all ranchers. Tabitha moved to a pew near the one they'd sat in the previous week. Alice was there and had saved a seat for her. "Thank you for not making me face all these people alone. I don't think I could tear Bert away from his friends if I tried."

"Oh, you couldn't. Men say women gossip, but I think men are worse than women most of the time."

Other women came over and introduced themselves, and after the third person, Tabitha leaned over to Alice. "We need to have a small party one day. Just so I can invite all the ladies over at once and get to know them better."

Alice wrinkled her nose. "They're easier to take individually. A group of women can be difficult to be around."

"I agree with you wholeheartedly," Tabitha said. "I'm glad I have you at my side for all these things. I may not have a mother-in-law but I'm glad I have you."

"I'm glad I have you too," Alice said. "Bert was smart when he married you. So glad he and Gladys never made it to the altar. That was a disaster waiting to happen."

Another woman stopped to meet Tabitha. "I'm Betty Gamble. My father is a rancher here in town. I didn't think anyone would ever agree to marry Bert."

Tabitha got to her feet. "I don't think there's anything at all wrong with Bert," she said.

"Oh, no, but he just doesn't seem compatible with women, does he?" Betty shook her head. "I do think he is just too forceful for most women. I hope he's gentle with you."

Tabitha was disgusted that the other woman would talk about her husband that way. She leaned forward so her lips were close to the other woman's ear. "I try to be gentle with him, but sometimes, I just can't help myself. Please don't ask him to see his bite marks."

Betty's eyes widened and she covered her mouth in shock. "I don't think we should be discussing things like that in church!"

"Just responding to the conversation you began," Tabitha said, moving to sit beside Alice. "I don't want to talk to you anymore. Go bother someone else."

After the odious woman had walked off, clearly offended, Tabitha felt Alice shaking beside her. "What?" Tabitha asked, refusing to back down from what she'd said. She looked over at Alice and saw the older woman was laughing.

"She's been trying to catch Bert's eye for years. I think that was her concession speech."

"It better have been. I want nothing else to do with her."

"What did you whisper to her?"

Tabitha blushed. "I told her I try to be gentle with Bert, but she shouldn't ask to see the bite marks."

Alice began laughing even harder. "I do love you, Tabitha Blander."

"And I love you," Tabitha said, joining in the laughter. "Maybe I went a bit too far with that."

"Not at all. I've been trying to get her to shut her mouth and walk away for years. You did it quickly. You deserve an award of some sort!"

Bert and George came over to sit down before the service. "What's so funny?" Bert asked.

Alice and Tabitha just laughed harder. "If anyone comes to you concerned about your welfare, it's all Alice's fault," Tabitha said, tears starting to stream down her face.

Bert and George exchanged a look. "It might be time to separate the two of them," George said.

"It's not," Alice said. "We just have similar senses of humor."

Bert looked at George. "That can't be good."

"I'm sure it's not!"

Tabitha elbowed Bert. "Shh...it's time for church."

Tabitha and Alice both had a hard time staying serious throughout the sermon. Something would strike one of them as funny, and they'd both laugh. Bert didn't look nearly as amused as Tabitha felt, though.

After church on the drive home, he asked, "What had you two so tickled during the service?"

Tabitha thought about it for a moment and decided to tell him everything. "Betty something or other introduced herself to me before church."

He groaned. "She's a menace."

"She said something about how surprising it is to see you married. She didn't think a woman would ever agree."

"That's ridiculous," he said. "She's had her pa approach me a dozen different times with the idea of the two of us marrying."

"I wondered if it wasn't something like that. She seemed to hate me from the moment we started talking." Tabitha shook her head. "She actually told me that she hoped you were gentle with me."

"There are words I want to call her that are not meant for mixed company. What did you tell her?"

"I told her I tried to be gentle with you, but she shouldn't ask to see your bite marks."

He looked at her with wide eyes for a moment, and then he started laughing. "Is that why you and Alice laughed through the whole sermon?"

Tabitha nodded. "I couldn't help myself. She stomped off after telling me I shouldn't say such things in church, but she started the whole thing." Tabitha sighed contentedly. "Usually I don't think of good retorts like that until it's too late. I was pretty proud of myself."

"I can see why you would be." He shook his head. "But you're right. What you said was deserved, and if she ever says anything like that to you again, I'll make sure she knows better."

"Thanks for not being angry with me about that," she said softly. "I really wasn't sure how you'd react, but Alice and I had fun with it."

"I think you did the right thing. Perhaps not in the right environment, but something like that needed to be said."

"You know, you're shaping up to be a halfway decent husband."

He shook his head. "It's a good thing I never expected obedience from you."

After lunch, he took her for a drive to see Jacob Small as she'd asked. When they got to where they could see the river, he pointed toward her. "That's him."

The man was at least fifty if he was a day, and he had a crook, like would be used with sheep. Instead, he was surrounded by pigs, and he was singing to them. His voice made her cringe. "I still feel I need to meet him," she said.

"All right." He drove down closer to the water's edge, and stopped at the side of the road there. "Let's go."

"You're going with me?" she asked, a little surprised.

"I may not be the gentlest husband in the world, but even I wouldn't let my wife go alone to meet a crazy man. And trust me. The man is crazy."

"I see that." She made her way down from the road to the bank of the river. "Hello!" she called loudly.

The man looked startled. "You a cattle rustler?" he asked.

"No, sir. I'm Tabitha. I came here to marry you."

The man took off his hat and scratched his head. "Well, that's mighty nice of ya, but I'm married to Mabel there." He used his thumb to point at a tree behind him. "You're too late."

"Did you send a letter to a matchmaker to find a wife?" she asked.

"Nope. Don't know who would have sent a letter like that."

"All right." The man didn't appear drunk to her, so he must truly be insane. "I guess I should be on my way then."

"Yep. I need to move the cattle to another pasture. This river likes to flood in the spring as all the snow melts."

"It does?"

"Oh, yes, it does."

"I brought you a few sandwiches if you'd like to have them."

"That would be right nice," he said, waiting for her to get the sandwiches. Then he saw Bert holding a small bag with the sandwiches in it. "How come you're with him if you came here to marry me?" he asked.

"You weren't there when I got here on the stagecoach, so this nice man told me he'd help me find a husband. Turned out that husband was him."

"You stole my wife?" Jacob asked, staring at Bert.

"I suppose I did, but you didn't seem to want her, or you'd have been there." Bert really wished he knew who had sent the letter to her.

"Just give me my sandwiches, and we'll call it even."

Bert happily handed the sandwiches over. He'd give the man sandwiches every week if that's what it took to keep Tabitha.

When he helped her back into the buggy, he could see that she was a little shocked at what they'd found. She waved at Jacob as they drove away. "Thank you for saving me from that."

Bert nodded. "Let's go on a real drive now, where our destination isn't a crazy old man who thinks his pigs are cows."

"Who feeds him normally?"

Bert shrugged. "Never really thought about it, but he definitely manages. He's thin but doesn't look like he's starving."

"Maybe he roasts one of the pigs every once in a while?"

"I guess it's possible."

He drove her through the entire area, pointing out different homes and buildings. "Was this area founded by settlers from the Oregon Trail?" he asked.

"Yup. Everything in this area was. All those people looking for free land. Can you imagine?"

"Don't even want to think about it," she said. "The land offices must have been crazy busy when wagon trains came through."

"Oh, they were. At least that's what my grandfather told me. My father was just a boy when they came, and he remembers very little of the journey, but my grandfather talked about it like it was a big adventure. My grandmother only talked about how hard it was."

"I have a feeling it was much harder for women than men. Women would have left behind everything they knew for a life of cooking over fires and keeping their kids from drowning in rivers. Men just drove and thought about the land they'd get." She shook her head. "I would not have wanted to be part of that. I'm usually up for any adventure, but you would have had to drag me kicking and screaming."

He chuckled. "I can't imagine you backing down from any kind of challenge." He stopped the wagon and got down, walking around to help her to her feet. "This is where the first settlers camped around here." Taking her hand, he pulled her to an area that was obviously once a huge campfire. "They cooked over this fire. They went all that way, wintered in Oregon, and then they came back this way in the spring, ready for a new life."

"I simply cannot imagine that much hardship."

"My grandmother kept a journal of the whole thing if you're inclined to read it. I tried once, but she talked about chores so much that I really got bored with it."

"I'd love to read it. Do you know where it is?"

"On the bookshelf in the parlor. I'll show you as soon as we get home. Grandmother was a grumpy old lady, but who wouldn't be after walking two thousand miles? I know I would."

Tabitha nodded, smiling. "I think I'd still be complaining my feet hurt."

He chuckled. "They got here in 1853. Hopefully, you wouldn't still be complaining."

"It's only been forty-five years then. You underestimate my ability to complain."

He pulled her to him, hugging her close. "Remind me to never give you any reason to complain then."

"Oh, you'll know it if you do." She grinned up at him. "We should get home. I need to make supper, and I have a feeling there will be other needs we should see to."

He laughed. "I do like the way you think, wife."

Chapter Nine

Tabitha had been in Wyoming a little over a month when a man came to the door. She opened it and didn't recognize the man as one of Bert's friends, and she certainly knew most of them—at least by sight. "May I help you?"

"Are you Tabitha Murphy?" he asked. The man was short, a couple inches shorter than Tabitha, and he wore a suit. His hair was bright red, and his eyes were brown.

"I was. Now I'm Tabitha Blander." Tabitha looked at the man in confusion.

"I sent off for a wife for my father, but I missed the stagecoach when it came in due to an accident. I've been trying to find you ever since."

"Are you Mr. Small then?"

The man nodded. "Jacob Small Jr. I live a few towns away, and I wanted someone here to look after my father."

Tabitha shrugged, not knowing exactly what to do. "I thought I had been abandoned. I married a kind man who asked, and I'm quite happy with him."

"But I paid for your train fare, and for your matchmaker to find you. Don't you think you should have been loyal to that?"

"I had my husband take me out to meet your father," Tabitha said. "He had no idea who I was, and he claimed a tree was his real wife. Then he traded me to the man I was already married to for three sandwiches. Your father doesn't need a wife, Mr. Small. He needs a caretaker."

"As that may be, I paid for you to come here to be his wife. You went back on our bargain. I will have to sue you for breach of promise."

Tabitha stared at the man in shock. "And as your father's wife, where would I live? Would I need to pretend the pigs he treats as sheep are really cattle?"

"You'd figure it out. Now, either come along with me, or I will get my lawyer involved."

"I'm afraid you'll need to get a lawyer involved," Tabitha said, thinking of the paltry amount of money she'd brought with her. She had no intention of asking Bert for money for her. He'd already traded three sandwiches for her after all.

"So be it." Mr. Small nodded to her as he walked toward his buggy. "If you'd been kinder, I may have offered myself up as a husband."

It was all Tabitha could do not to laugh at that comment. He didn't hold a candle to her Bert.

As soon as the man was gone, Tabitha turned around to see Alice standing there, frowning at her. "We'll tell Bert what happened as soon as he gets home," Alice said.

Tabitha shook her head. "No, I don't think that would be wise. I have some money I saved and brought with me. I will just pray it's enough."

Alice shook her head. "That's not going to work. Bert will be very upset if you don't at least talk to him about it."

"Maybe he will, but that doesn't mean I'm going to talk to him about it. Instead, I'll handle this on my own."

"All right. I'll wait a little while before I talk to him."

For the next day or two, Tabitha prayed a lot about what was going to happen even as her mind was working on ways to make some money, so she could handle the court case on her own.

Finally, on Saturday afternoon, she sat down with Alice. "Are there any bachelors in the area who would enjoy a homecooked meal?" Tabitha asked. "I could make them here, and deliver them to the men, then pick up their dirty dishes after."

"That's a terrible idea," Alice said. "You'd be alone with bachelors. I think you should just talk to Bert."

"But this isn't his problem. He traded three sandwiches for me. Of course, I made the sandwiches, so I don't know that they were his to trade."

"You're silly." Alice frowned. "Could you agree to take a meal to Mr. Small's father twice a week? Would that appease the son?"

"I have no idea. I wouldn't mind that, to be honest. Mr. Small Senior is a very nice man. Confused, but kind. I wonder if we could take him some meals and give him a place—like the barn—to wait out storms. Would that be enough?"

"I don't know. I'm not the type of person who would leave someone after they got off a stagecoach, and then expect them to marry the person I told them to marry, so I have no idea. Perhaps it would work. It's already cold enough that he needs a place to stay. Maybe you could take him warm clothes and some food."

"Maybe I could." Tabitha nodded. "I'll make him a nice homecooked meal and have Bert drive me down to the river to deliver it. And then I can work on a heavy shirt or even a coat this week and take it to him next week."

Alice nodded. "I think that's a much better idea than you driving around taking bachelors their meals. We know that Mr. Small Senior is harmless."

"I'll get started on some mittens for him now. I believe I can have some ready by tomorrow, and I'll take him some of what I cook for us at Sunday dinner. That should keep his son at bay for at least a few days."

"That sounds good. But I really do think you should tell Bert what's going on. He would be happy to pay the man off."

"I just don't want him to have to spend his hard-earned money. That should be his to do what he wishes to do."

"I think he would strongly disagree."

Tabitha was just putting supper on the table when Bert came in at the end of his day. He looked exhausted. "I'm glad tomorrow is our day of rest," she said.

He nodded. "I am as well. I may even skip church so I can sleep all day."

"I was hoping you'd take me for a drive down by the river. I made some mittens for Mr. Small today, and I thought I'd take him a meal as well."

Bert groaned. "You are not beholden to that man."

"Of course, I'm not, but I can show him kindness, can't I?"

"Kindness is always a good thing." He yawned. "I'll drive you down after church."

"Then we'll sleep the rest of the day away."

He pulled her against him. "And I can have my way with you all afternoon?" he asked.

She laughed. "I suppose you can."

AT CHURCH THE NEXT day, Tabitha's eyes scanned the crowd, hoping she wouldn't see either of the Mr. Smalls. Thankfully, neither was there. She dreaded the idea of running into the young Mr. Small with Bert around. She was afraid Bert would take matters into his own hands. He had a reputation for having a temper, though she hadn't seen it since the day they met, and that was more amusement than temper.

Alice knew what Tabitha was doing, and whispered, "Just tell him."

Tabitha shook her head. It wasn't so much that she was ashamed she'd married Bert instead of Jacob. It was that she didn't want him to have to waste his money to get her out of a lawsuit. No, instead, she'd simply deal with the matter on her own.

She had Jacob's meal in the buggy, planning to head down to the river straight after church. It would give Bert more time to rest afterward.

As they left the church, Betty grabbed her shoulder. "I've heard you've had tea with all the ladies in town. I'm a lady."

Tabitha smiled sweetly. "You are a woman in town, yes. I don't plan to invite you for tea, though. You haven't been exactly kind."

Betty huffed and followed her to the buggy. "You can't say things like that to me."

Bert stopped and looked at Betty. "I think you need to remember that Tabitha is my wife, and as such, she deserves respect. Please don't say another word to her."

Betty crossed her arms over her chest, but the look of disgust on her face wasn't surprising to anyone who looked at her. She had a reputation in town for being very difficult to deal with.

Bert helped Tabitha into the buggy, kissing her as he did so. Tabitha knew the kiss was just to make Betty mad, so she participated in the kiss as much as she could. When he let her go and walked around the wagon, she knew he was happy with her. Betty didn't belong in either of their lives.

Driving down to the river was more difficult than it had been a month earlier, when there had not been any snow. The river bank was frozen, though the water still flowed.

Jacob Small was there, herding his pigs. "Well, hello!" he called out.

Tabitha got down from the buggy, carrying the meal and the mittens as well. "I brought you some food." It was in a burlap sack, so she was able to hand it off easily. "There's fried chicken and baked potatoes in there." And then she handed him the pure red mittens she'd made. "And I thought this might keep your hands warm."

"You're the lady I traded for three sandwiches!" Jacob said, his face lighting up as he realized who she was.

"I am. Is there anything else you need?"

Jacob shook his head. "I'm just happy for the meal and the mittens. Thank you."

"You're very welcome. Are you building fires at night to keep warm?"

He nodded. "If I get too cold, I find a barn to stay in."

"You're always welcome in our barn," she told him as she turned to walk back to the buggy. "I'll bring you food again, if you'd like."

Jacob nodded. "The wife's not a very good cook. She's too busy waving her hands around saying silly things." He whispered loudly, "I think she might be insane."

Tabitha stifled the giggle that wanted to break free. "She might be."

As she and Bert drove away, she could see Jacob was looking at his tree wife contemplatively. As if he was trying to decide if he needed to get some help for her insanity.

"I feel much better about myself now that I've done that," she said. "Now, let's go home and eat!"

"I'm pretty hungry!"

They had fried chicken and mashed potatoes for lunch, along with some green beans. "Is this what you took Jacob?" Bert asked.

"I took him fried chicken and baked potatoes. I didn't think mashed potatoes would do well in a burlap sack, and I don't want to lose dishes by dropping them off to him, and him losing them."

"Makes sense. Your gravy is absolutely delicious. I think he'd give me back those three sandwiches if he knew just how good of a cook you are."

Tabitha laughed. "I'm not so sure of that. He did trade happily."

"That's true..."

"Should we find an asylum to take him in?"

"I think if he was starving or if he was a danger to others, that would be fine. But right now, he's simply odd. I don't think he needs an asylum yet."

"All right," Tabitha said skeptically. The man seemed like he needed to have someone care for him, and she wasn't about to be the one to do it. Helping him with small things made her happy, though.

They spent the rest of the day sleeping and eating and enjoying one another. They even spent some time in the parlor reading, which had become a regular thing to do on Sundays. Polly rested beside Tabitha on the sofa. The kitten had to be right up next to her and touching her whenever she could.

Several times, Tabitha's mind wandered from the book she was reading to her predicament, and then she'd find herself studying Bert. How on earth would he react when he found out she was being sued?

Her reputation would be ruined, and there was no doubt about that. Would he have a problem being married to a woman whose reputation was in tatters?

Finally, not long before bedtime, she found the words coming out of her mouth. "Bert?"

He looked at her over the top of his book. "Yes?"

She took a deep breath, needing to purge the secret from her conscience. "Jacob Smith Junior came to see me this week. He's the one who paid for me to come here, but an emergency came up, and he couldn't meet me at the stagecoach."

Bert looked at her for a moment. "You were supposed to marry a different Jacob Small?"

She shook her head. "No, I was supposed to marry the one we thought. He was basically asking me to be a caretaker for his father. He says he's going to sue me for breach of promise."

"Didn't he promise to meet you at the stagecoach?" Bert asked. "That's the only reason you broke your promise. You thought you'd been lured out here and left on your own."

"I told him that, but he didn't agree." She sighed. "I don't want my reputation ruined, but I'm not going to divorce you to marry a crazy man. I will give him a little more help because his son did pay for my journey here, but…I'm happy married to you. I wouldn't be to him."

"No, of course you wouldn't." Bert frowned. "Let the son take us to court. I'll pay whatever the fine the judge comes up with, but I think Jacob Small Senior has a right to be at the trial, don't you?"

"Are you angry with me?" she asked.

"I do wish you'd told me sooner, but that would be a hard thing to do. So no, I'm not angry. We'll work through this together."

Tabitha stood and walked over to Bert sitting on his lap in the armchair he preferred. "Thank you," she said softly, kissing him.

"Don't ever be afraid to tell me when something goes wrong," he told her. "We're a team now that we're married. If something is happening to you, it's happening to me as well."

She nodded, tears in her eyes. "I was afraid to tell you. I don't want you to have to spend money just to keep my reputation intact."

"Don't worry about the money. We can handle it."

"Well, that depends how much we're being sued for, doesn't it?"

"Trust me, we can handle it."

Polly jumped over to them then, sitting on Bert's chest. She obviously felt her place in the family was between them.

They both laughed when she started rubbing her face on Bert's shirt, hoping to get some ear scratches. Having a kitten was the best thing Tabitha could think of.

Chapter Ten

Two weeks later, Bert and Tabitha went to court, which was held right there in the church where they were married. She didn't know if she should be embarrassed or not, but there weren't a lot of people in court that day.

Bert had decided to stop and get Mr. Small Senior from his spot near the river. He ate the sandwiches Tabitha had packed for them on the way to court. "You sure do make a fine sandwich," he told her with his mouth full.

"Thank you," she said softly, pleased he was always so happy with her cooking.

He sat with them on a pew, and when his son came over to get him to sit with him, he said, "This lady brings me food. You just bring me disappointment." Jacob turned his head away from his son and smiled at Tabitha. "I sure did like that fried chicken."

It was then that Tabitha realized he was wearing the mittens she'd made for him and the matching scarf they'd taken him just a week before.

When the judge called the court to session, Tabitha found she was more nervous than she would have liked. Her character was on trial here more than anything else.

Bert had hired an attorney to defend her, but she had a feeling it wouldn't do a lot of good.

First, the attorney for Jacob Junior opened stating that Tabitha had come west under false pretenses, and she had conned Jacob Junior into paying her way. Bert almost came out of his seat a few times, wanting to argue with the lawyer, but the defense lawyer would simply shake his head and Bert would sit back down.

Tabitha could feel him getting more upset by the minute. "We'll have our say," she told him.

Finally, as Jacob Junior was on the stand and answering questions, Jacob Senior stood up. He seemed to have just realized what the trial was about.

He walked to the front of the church and looked at his son. "I'm ashamed of you. I already have a wife, and I don't need another."

"Father, your wife is a tree!"

"She looks over me and keeps me happy. What more could a man want?"

The lawyers both seemed to be startled as Jacob talked to his son in front of the church the way he was doing.

"I paid for Tabitha Murphy to come west and marry you. She didn't. It's that simple."

"Why was I never told I was supposed to marry her?"

"You don't listen to me when I visit. You just keep calling your pigs cows and carrying that shepherd stick."

"I asked if I could live with you every time you came to visit me. And every time you refused. And now you think you can force me to marry a woman against my will? Well, it won't work. I traded her for three sandwiches, and it was the best trade I ever made."

The judge narrowed his eyes. "Did you ever want to marry Mrs. Blander?" he asked.

Jacob shook his head. "I wouldn't have traded her for three sandwiches if I had, now, would I?"

"I suppose not."

"Besides, even without being married to me, she brings me food, and these nice mittens. And this scarf!" He lifted the scarf from his chest. "Best bargain I ever made. If he wants to bring me another wife, I'll trade her for sandwiches too."

There was laughter from the few people in the church. Jacob's lawyer looked utterly embarrassed. "I'd like to call Mrs. Blander to the stand."

Bert squeezed Tabitha's hand as she walked to the front of the church and sat in the chair indicated. After she was sworn in, the questions started. "Did you agree to come west to marry the elder Mr. Small?"

Tabitha nodded. "I did, but—"

"We're not looking for a story. Just answer the question," the lawyer said. "And when you arrived did you marry Mr. Blander within twenty-four hours."

"Yes, I did." She bit her tongue as she wanted to say more, but she knew the lawyer would just interrupt again.

"And before the younger Mr. Small went to your house, did you make any effort to meet with the elder Mr. Small?"

"I did."

"You did?" the lawyer asked, looking confused. "But you didn't marry him?"

"I was already married when I went to introduce myself to him. He made it clear he had no desire to marry me, and he was happily married to an oak tree." Tabitha felt like she'd won a small battle when he didn't interrupt her comments.

"Why didn't you tell the younger Mr. Small that you had done so when he came to your home?"

"I did."

The lawyer was now glaring at his client. "You told him you had met his father?"

"Yes, and I even told him that his father traded me for three sandwiches."

"I have no further questions," the lawyer said, moving to sit down, obviously annoyed at the turn his case was taking.

The defense lawyer stood. "When you arrived here, why did you not immediately marry Mr. Small?"

Tabitha sighed. "No one came to meet me at the stagecoach which were the prior arrangements we'd made. I thought I was stranded here, and I had no desire to go home."

"And what happened next?"

"Mr. Blander was walking by, and I asked him about Mr. Small. He told me many things about Mr. Small, and I realized he simply wouldn't be a suitable husband for me, and Mr. Blander asked me to marry him instead. I made the choice to marry Mr. Blander, and I'm happily married to him now, seven weeks later."

"How long was it between the day you arrived and the day the younger Mr. Small came to your door?"

"Five weeks. I don't know what I would have done if I hadn't married Mr. Blander. I would have been completely alone over a thousand miles from my parents. I knew no one."

"Did he tell you why he wasn't there the day you arrived? Or why it took him five weeks to come see you?"

"No, he didn't give any reasons. He just started threatening me." Tabitha noticed that the younger Mr. Small was sinking down in his seat. "I believe him leaving me at the stagecoach was breach of promise, was it not?"

"It most certainly was." Her lawyer looked at the judge. "I have no further questions."

The judge frowned. "I have a question."

"What's that?" Tabitha asked.

"Did you take food and clothing to Mr. Small because you felt guilty for not marrying him?"

"Not at all. I took him food and clothing because he is a kind man who lives all alone. I thought if I could make his day just a little bit better, then I should."

"You may take your seat, Mrs. Blander." The judge shook his head. "I would like for both lawyers to approach the bench."

Tabitha moved back to her seat beside Bert, and she clutched his hand tightly as she waited for what the judge would have to say about it all.

Finally, the lawyers left, but the smile on her lawyer's face told her everything.

"I believe after hearing from all sides that Mrs. Blander did the only thing she could do when she married Mr. Blander. The only person here who is in breach of promise is Mr. Small. Now, I wouldn't usually have a problem with a man who had an emergency and didn't show up to greet his future stepmother, but the younger Mr. Small made this my business. I have fined him for the amount of my travel here, and I will ask that he pay to Mrs. Blander the equivalent of five weeks in a boarding house. I will have the figure sent to you, Mr. Small."

The younger Mr. Small stood up to protest. "That's not fair, judge. She's the one who married someone else."

"I won't hear another word from you, Mr. Small." Then the judge turned to the elder Mr. Small. "Do you need a place to live? There are places who will take good care of you."

"My wife and I do fine with our cattle. If my son ever decides to let me live with him, I won't say no, but I would still spend the summers with my wife and cattle."

The judge smiled. "Well, then we'll let you stay where you're happy. Do you need a ride home?"

Mr. Small shook his head. "No, Mr. and Mrs. Blander will take me home. They are very kind to me. Much kinder than my son has ever been."

The judge nodded. "Isn't it nice to have such good neighbors?" he asked.

"It certainly is. But I ate all my sandwiches on the way here."

"Is there anyone in town who runs a café or makes meals for others?"

Bert stood. "There isn't, but if he'd like to come home with us for the night, we'd be happy to feed him." Then he smiled. "I guess I should ask my wife if she's willing to feed him first, shouldn't I?"

"I would think so," the judge said. "Court dismissed." He pounded his little gavel and they all stood to leave.

When Mr. Small joined them at the back of the church, Tabitha asked, "Would you like to come home with us for a night? I'd feed you supper and then breakfast tomorrow, and my husband would take you home."

Mr. Small shook his head. "No, but I'll come by when it gets too cold to sleep outside, if that's all right."

Tabitha nodded. "That's fine. And I'll bring you some more food after church on Sunday."

Mr. Small stopped walking and took Tabitha's hand. "Trading you for those sandwiches is the smartest thing I've ever done."

Tabitha laughed. "You just let me know what your favorite meal is, and I'll be sure to bring it."

LATER THAT EVENING, after they'd had supper, Bert grinned at Tabitha. "Our day in court was more than I could have asked for."

"I agree. I can't believe the judge decided that Mr. Small owes us money. That was crazy." Tabitha shook her head. "And it didn't seem to hurt my reputation at all. No one was really there but the judge, lawyers, both Mr. Smalls, and us."

"I'm glad it was so easy. Now I just have to work twice as hard tomorrow," he said.

"Did you see the judge's face when the older Mr. Small told the court that he'd traded me for three sandwiches? I'd told his son that, but he didn't believe me."

Bert laughed. "My three-sandwich bride. Who would have thought I'd get off so cheaply and end up married to the woman of my dreams."

"Woman of your dreams?" she asked. "Did you decide I was that before or after I kicked you?"

He grinned. "After of course. I could never marry a woman who couldn't stand up to me and fight with me for what she wanted."

She shook her head. "You're insane, Bert Blander. I think that may be why I love you so much."

He looked at her for a moment. "You love me? Don't say it if it isn't true!"

"It's very true," she told him. "I've loved you since I met with Gladys. Though why that showed me how wonderful you are, I'll never know."

"I've loved you since you kicked me and told me to stop laughing at you. Marrying you was the best decision I ever made. Though once I kissed you, the decision was out of my hands."

She moved to sit on his lap again, her little shadow kitten jumping to sit between them. "If you love me then you won't be terribly disappointed with the news I have."

"News?" he asked.

"I'm expecting. I've suspected for a few days, but now I'm certain."

"A baby? Already?" He stared at her in disbelief for a moment.

"I'm not sure why you're surprised. It's not like we never make love..."

He grinned. "I guess a baby is to be expected." He shook his head. "I really didn't think it would happen so soon. My mother tried for years to have me. When she finally was expecting, she was extremely excited."

"I don't blame her. She had a mighty fine son too."

He pulled her a little closer, making Polly squawk. As they kissed, it was as if all of the hardships in the world disappeared. They were definitely better together than they were apart.

"I'm going to be a father," he said, still a little stunned.

"Yes, you definitely are."

Epilogue

It was late July when the baby finally came. Alice acted as midwife, as she had for Bert's birth. Tabitha's pains came early on a Monday morning, and the women decided together to not tell the men until they were home from work. Alice said she had no desire to have Bert and George underfoot all day.

It was shortly after lunchtime when the baby made her way into the world. Tabitha kept staring at her daughter, not sure how she came to be. Tabitha had expected a son. Sons couldn't be traded for sandwiches. But she had a girl.

They'd only picked out boys' names, so she had no idea what to call the little miracle she held in her arms. "What was Bert's mother's name?" Tabitha asked Alice who was still cleaning up the bed.

"Cassandra," Alice said. "She was called Cassie by her friends."

"Cassandra." Tabitha repeated the name a few times, trying to decide if it was too big a name for the tiny human she held. "We could call her Candy."

Alice smiled. "I like that. Cassandra Ann?"

"No, I think Cassandra Lynn. It just flows off the tongue. Now how am I going to tell Bert we had a girl? Both of us have been thinking it was a boy all along."

Alice laughed. "That little girl is going to have her daddy wrapped around her finger. He will love her instantly and forever."

"You think?"

"I know."

Sure enough, when Bert came in after work that evening, he walked into the parlor where Tabitha was sitting holding the baby. He stopped, his eyes widening. "You didn't send someone to tell me the baby was on the way?" he asked, seeming upset.

"Alice and I decided we didn't need men underfoot," she said. "Everything went perfectly. Go wash that mud off your hands, and I'll let you hold her."

"Her?" Bert looked like he was choking. "It's a girl?"

"I want to name her Cassandra Lynn, after your mother."

For a moment, her big, tall cowboy looked as if he was about to cry. "I'll go wash my hands."

He hurried away, and when he came back a minute later, he looked more composed. Sitting beside her on the sofa, he reached out and traced the baby's tiny cheek. "She's beautiful. Just like her mother."

Tabitha laughed, though tears did fall down her cheeks. "I was so sure we were having a boy."

"But God gave us the most beautiful baby in the world. Who could ask for more?"

Don't miss out!

Visit the website below and you can sign up to receive emails whenever Kirsten Osbourne publishes a new book. There's no charge and no obligation.

https://books2read.com/r/B-A-VSFD-BPQKC

BOOKS 2 READ

Connecting independent readers to independent writers.